Bright Stars
In a
Big Sky

BigSky Writers

To Lauren with my
very best wishes

Copyright © 2017 BigSky Writers

ISBN: 1978304528

ISBN-13: 978-1978304529

Cover design by Daphne deMuir
Original photograph by Nicola McDonagh

This book is dedicated to one of our writers, Anne Foster-Clarke, who, despite a very difficult year has supported and contributed to producing our latest edition.

CONTENTS

A BRITISH EXIT
Will Ingrams

'Hello?' Cynthia powered herself towards the door of the breakfast room, puzzled by the silence in the lodge. No response.

'Jessica? Vera? Where is everyone?' She steered the motorised chair awkwardly through the opening, feeling unsettled. There was no-one there.

Cyn guided her chariot round the large table, which was bare and wiped clean. She peered through the floor-to-ceiling window at the salted road below, a black stripe between grey slush and the mounds of brilliant snow heaped at its sides. No-one around. Very strange.

She heard a tread on the stairs, and a man's voice reached the dining room ahead of him, 'Oh, God! Don't say I'm too late!'

Alarm clutched at Cynthia and a thought shivered free - they'd left the resort without her!

Anthony hurried through the doorway, peered round the room and spotted Cynthia by the glass. 'You too? Have they left us both behind?'

'Looks like it,' Cyn grunted, pulling a wry expression as she nodded to the man she had mentally dubbed Anxious Ant.

'I'm sure I set my alarm - I remember moving the tiny hand to just before six. Maybe I didn't raise the button completely. Oh, Lord. Whatever now?'

Cyn watched Anthony's hands clutching each other, fingers twisting nervously. He was a tall man who had to duck his head to get on and off the coach, but he lived in a bubble of hesitancy, permanently unsure of what to do next. Weak, thought Cyn, despite the strength of his features - thick eyebrows, prominent nose.

'Can you remember the schedule, Anthony?' She pushed the button to drive herself towards him, 'What time does the train leave?'

Anthony stopped wringing his hands and turned his left palm up to peer at a thin watch worn inside his wrist. Illogical and unnecessary, Cyn thought. She could see the current time, ten past seven, on the wall clock, and so could he.

'Er, eight forty something, I think,' he

stuttered, struggling with inner despair.

'Surely the coach can't take that long?,' Cynthia mused, 'Why such an early start?'

'Breakfast at the station, Cynthia. Don't you remember?' Anthony spoke distractedly, eyes searching the room as if the rest of their party might be hiding behind the curtains. 'Frau Schlegel couldn't offer breakfast this morning - the season finished yesterday, and the staff have already left. I watched Pedro lugging his suitcase down the road last night.'

'Well, nobody told me! I thought it would all be the same as usual. Ridiculous!' Then Cynthia's face cleared, 'I can imagine why they left without *me* - Jessica probably arranged a taxi, because she knows I can't get up the steps of the coach. But why didn't they miss you, Anthony?'

'I can't think.' Then he gasped and raised a hand to his forehead, 'Oh Lord, yes I can!' Anthony bit at his knuckle. 'That church - the elegant one with the tall spire, down in the town - I told Jessica I'd like to photograph it in the dawn light, without all the traffic. She assumed I'd gone on ahead. Oh Lord!'

'Hm. Plausible. But where's my taxi, then?

And where on earth's Frau Schlegel?'

Anthony was lost in worry and self-recrimination, as if a logical explanation made things worse. The others had gone. They were abandoned.

'Right! Time for action. We can still catch that train if we get a move on.' Cynthia took charge. 'Anthony, you go and fetch our luggage. My suitcase is propping my door open - just beyond the lift. I'll beetle around down here for signs of life, right? Off you go!'

As he turned for the stairs, Cynthia powered her scooter down the carpetted corridor, motor whining. The reception area was deserted, security grill down, and there was no response to her calls. She rolled past the locked office to try Frau Schlegel's quarters - her bunker, as Vera put it - but the door was locked and hammering brought no answer. She returned to the lift and waited for Anthony to descend.

Cyn had actually enjoyed the Alpine Winter Wonders holiday. She'd almost cancelled when her right knee went out in sympathy with her left hip, leaving her reliant upon mechanical conveyance. Happily her fear of being the pariah, the cripple, had proved groundless.

Jessica had done her best to deliver the brochure's accessibility promises, and most of the party had been helpful without condescension. She may have delayed them all at times - ramps sought, steps avoided - but she'd heard very few moans and tuts. Vera's comment about extermination had actually been a lighthearted Dalek reference rather than a proposal of euthanasia.

And now this. Anthony was an unpromising sidekick, but she'd drive some iron into his soul. The lift doors opened to reveal his stooped back, hands reaching toward the cases.

'My phone fell from the funicular yesterday, as you may recall, Anthony. Have you got yours handy?'

The tall man turned to apologise, straightening between the lift doors, 'Sorry, Cynthia. I didn't get roaming enabled - what with the exorbitant charges, and everyone else having phones...'

Cyn grunted. 'So, no mobile, and the office phone's locked behind the grill! We can't call Jessica. Or a taxi. We'll just have to find some transport for ourselves, won't we?'

Anthony struggled the suitcases out of the

lift towards the front entrance of the deserted lodge while Cynthia slapped the square panel to open the doors and drove through. She gasped at the chill air that bit her nose and caught in her throat, pausing on the zig-zag ramp to fasten the buttons of her cardigan in the pure, crisp silence. Jagged white peaks gazed down with a pervasive calm that she would normally have welcomed.

Fresh snow had dusted things during the night, but the heavily salted paths and roadways were clear. The village was unnaturally peaceful this morning - no noisy tangles of skiers heading for the lifts, no steaming exhausts as drivers warmed car engines, no buses quivering as they idled. The car park to her left held only two vehicles - a large dark Mercedes lightly covered from the night's snowfall, and a small three-wheeled utility truck with its tailgate down and a clear windscreen revealing an empty cab. End of the season. Deserted.

A scraping and muttering made her glance back at the door. Anthony with the bags. He was wreathed in breath-steam and pressed a hand into his back as he straightened, grimacing. The cases stood side by side, patiently waiting.

'Run down to the road, Anthony. See if you can spot a taxi or something. You'll be quicker than me.'

Anthony frowned at the thought of running, but he nodded rapidly and scrabbled off with an urgent but ungainly stiff-legged walk, rather like a spider with six of its legs missing. Not an athlete.

Cyn rolled down the second section of ramp and followed him towards the main street, the road that climbed from the distant town past all the hotels and lodges to end at the ski lifts and surrounding chalets. Before she was halfway there, however, she stopped to hear Anthony's report, shouted back from the corner. The motor's whine obliterated his first words.

'..I'm afraid. Quite deserted, actually. Oh, wait! There's a taxi coming up the hill. Thank goodness!'

'Get in the road and flag him down, man!' Cynthia called back, waving him forward, 'If he can't take us, he can radio for one that can!'

The thin, brittle air carried voices swiftly - Anthony's progress was slower. Cynthia watched him nervously negotiate the heaped and frozen slush at the kerb to stand flamingo-like in the road, waving both arms over his head.

'No!' he shouted, 'Up here!' Cynthia watched him stagger forward and disappear down the road, out of sight. Her motor whirred up again as she rolled forward, hoping to discover Anthony in conversation with a taxi driver. But no. She heard his desperate shouts peter out with distance and fading conviction before she saw his distant shape, bent over and struggling for foggy breath, with a tiny dark car turning the corner a good way beyond and below the hopeless man.

She didn't expect Ant to return quickly, and their need for transport was urgent, so she turned her front wheels uphill and set off to seek help. The beauty of the unpeopled resort struck her - timeless jagged peaks guarding cascades of fir trees, dark where they had shed the snow, with clear bright runs snaking down to the charming frost-topped chalets and lodges. So calm and unmoved.

The next building on her right was hoisting a thin trail of smoke into the clear air - surely it was inhabited. Cynthia turned onto the path leading to its door, raising a hand to alert Anthony. It was a house rather than a hotel, but she knew that every building in the village hosted visitors at peak times. She couldn't reach the door - there was a step and no ramp - but she hammered on the large window nearby.

She heard nothing and saw no movement, but Cyn was convinced that someone was inside. She pummelled again, and was rewarded with an indistinct shout and, after a pause, a pale shape approached, growing rapidly behind the obscure glass like an inflating life raft. The door swung away and Cynthia gasped to see an enormous peeled pear of a man - it was as if God's large hand had squeezed his head and shoulders into insignificance and squirted their volume into his lower portions. A buttermilk dressing gown covered his shoulders without hope of girdling his lardy hips and elephantine alabaster legs.

'Ja? Was ist los?' The voice that escaped the fronds of his pale droopy moustache was surprisingly high and puny for so large a man.

Cynthia was not up to German conversation this morning, and spoke English, slowly and with forceful clarity, 'Help. Station. Taxi.' She added, 'Bitte?'

The bleached mountain before her gazed down without apparent understanding, and raised his finger to pause the moment before retreating ponderously. Cynthia heard an exchange in German and the behemoth was replaced by a twiggy person clutching a fake fur coat to her bones in the chilly draft of the open door. Frau Schlegel.

'Oh! Miss Cynthia, you are still here?'

'They left without me, Frau Schlegel,' Cyn replied, disappointed to sound so pitiful, almost tearful. 'My taxi didn't come. I don't know why...'

'Ah, I am knowing all about it - the reason for the not coming.' She paused, perhaps considering either stepping outside or hauling Cynthia indoors, but realised that neither would be practical. She re-wrapped herself with a shiver and continued.

'There is, starting today, in the next valley, the EU Summit Meeting to discuss the exit of the British. All taxis will be at the station and at the airport. It is better money for them I think.'

'But we have to leave!'

'I know this. You all make the ridiculous vote, last June, no?'

'No! I mean Anthony and me! We have to catch the train!'

'Mister Anthony also? Where is he please?'

The male peacock has a piercing yet mournful call. Something similar in a more desperate, lower register seized their attention, and they turned to see a significant cloud of vapour approaching with the flailing and wheezing Anthony at its core.

'So, the autobus has gone and your train will depart at eight forty seven, this I believe. We cannot bring for you a taxi to the Bahnhof. Also you have this chair with the wheels and Mister Anthony.'

During this summary the man himself floundered up to them and sat slumped and steaming on the step.

Frau Schlegel studied both of the would-be leavers in turn, then announced brightly, 'I have the answer - Rudi!' She turned to shout instructions toward the bedroom, eventually gaining a grumpy assent.

'My friend Rudi - he has the klein lastwagen!' She pointed down, through the wall, towards the lodge car park. Cynthia peered over her shoulder at the dark Mercedes below. Then she realised that Frau Schlegel referred to the three-wheeled delivery truck.

Five minutes later all four of them were in the car park and Rudi, nimble as an overweight scout tent, was attaching long steel ramps to the truck's tailgate. Cynthia's erstwhile landlady, now with several insulating layers under her buttoned coat, hastened him. Anthony hovered to one side, fingers fluttering, as the ascent began with a short run-up under Rudi's magisterial gaze. Cyn knew she had to rush the ramps if the scooter was to make it to the top, despite her terror and the battery's uncertain state of charge. She gritted her teeth, gripped tightly and prayed to stay straight as her height above the hard glistening tarmac grew alarmingly.

The front wheels crested the ramp ends and dropped gently onto the bed of the pickup while the rear wheels still climbed, but then the underside grated - there was insufficient clearance. Rudi lurched forward to lift and push, and Anthony wafted ineffectually while the wheels slipped and spun. Cyn solved the problem herself by leaning forward and rocking the machine, a scary undertaking, until she shot forward into the back wall of the cab. She sat back heavily and released the drive button, gasping with relief while the truck rocked on its springs. Anthony struggled their suitcases over the sides as Rudi clattered the ramps away and raised the tailgate.

Frau Schlegel ran to the lodge to fetch a blanket for the prominently-perched Cynthia, and Anthony went to climb into the cab. This was a mistake. Rudi had already squeezed his bulky regions through the inadequate door, and was massaging them past the steering column in a practised manner. Once the quivering ceased, the whole bench seat was occupied by indefinable masses of fundamental Rudi and no amount of folding would have fitted Anthony into there too.

Rudi jerked his thumb over his shoulder and Anthony, with the assistance of a mudguard and a contorted landlady, toppled awkwardly over the side to lodge by the tailgate. Cyn patted his head indulgently then waved a gloved hand to Frau Schlegel and reached forward to slap the roof of the cab, spurring on their canned driver.

The engine fired, sounding more like a wasp exploring an empty Coke can than a credible source of motive power for this weighty load. Cyn re-draped her blanket to shelter the pulsing Anthony, but Rudi's engine stalled when he dropped the clutch, leaving them all rocking in steam and silence. A whine and a more conservative start, saw them leave the fur-wrapped frau and sway across the car park to the road.

Cynthia's head topped the roof of the cab by a couple of imperial feet, and once they turned downhill and picked up speed through the icy air things became distinctly unpleasant. Her eyes began to water, then stream, and the tears froze, crackling the skin at her temples and in her hair. Breathing pained her nostrils and made her teeth ache. Anthony, having cooled from his climb, shivered violently and moaned quietly, tugging more of the blanket around himself.

The glorious scenery - a pale sun now breaking through skeins of silvery cloud between the peaks - was ignored. Cyn had her eyes closed tight and Ant was invisible beneath clutched rug. The long descent through the deserted village was almost straight and increasingly rapid, so their reckless approach to the junction with the four lane highway failed to alarm the passengers at all. It was Rudi, desperately applying all the brakes he had, who realised he couldn't bring this momentous load to a timely halt on this slope.

Cyn didn't recognised the German for *Hold Tight!*, but Rudi's reedy tone of alarm and the sideways slewing and tipping alerted her to their peril. It was a right turn, so fortunately they did not have to cross a stream of traffic - merely join one. Rudi struggled to steer a fine line between careering across two highway lanes to smash into the central concrete barrier and toppling his overladen lastwagen onto its port side with the loss of all aboard. They skidded across the inside lane on two wheels, passing between a Latvian container truck and a long transporter bearing eleven Nissans manufactured in Sunderland, to join the fast lane in the path of a hooting and flashing BMW Seven Series saloon. They didn't exactly stay upright, but a light bounce off the central barrier set them back on their wheels, though the little truck continued to sway and meander for several hundred metres.

The highway traffic continued to race on towards the town, generally unaware that a small vehicle with three mismatched occupants had been recklessly inserted into its midst. As they approached the Bahnhof turnoff Cynthia even considered whether Rudi had planned that appalling manoeuvre as a time-saver. Certainly, it now seemed that they might catch the train with the others - the station clock was showing eight-forty when it slipped into sight between the tall office blocks among whose roots the slip road had delivered them.

The final mishap occurred as Rudi turned them into the station plaza. A very similar utility truck to theirs, but laden with bins of rubbish and sweepings from the concourse, was rumbling and rocking over the cobbles as they arrived. Although their speed was now moderate, Rudi's vehicle remained overloaded and unstable. The two three-wheelers would have passed each other cleanly had a small brown dog not sniffed its way back into their path. Rudi swerved to avoid the dachshund, and the swaying load bed battered the side of the refuse cart.

With a clatter that echoed across the plaza, round lids slid off the metal dustbins, one of them toppling over Anthony's concealed form and rolling to rest beside Cynthia's chariot. At the same time the broom that had stood between them, brush head uppermost, fell towards her and Cyn had to grab it. Thrusting out her hand dislodged the blanket and draped from her shoulder as Rudi, cursing dog and driver, rumbled them towards the station portico. Cynthia, relieved, felt a rush of gratitude towards their saviours - despite the handicap of being European, Rudi and Frau Schlegel had delivered them intact and on time.

The little truck shuddered to a halt before a crowd of smartly dressed EU politicians and assistants waiting impatiently for more taxis to carry them to their unwelcome discussions. The startled delegates looked up at Cynthia on her dais, her vertical broom and borrowed cloak arrayed behind a battered shield, and recognised the image of a shabby, defiant Britannia. Her divided grey helmet of hair and the sharp nose looked strangely familiar.

Anthony's head popped out of the drapery

just as Jessica scurried from the far entrance, waving impatiently. She bellowed, for all the world to hear, 'Hurry up, you two, we're leaving! Anyone would think you wanted to remain here!'

THE CHRISTMAS STAR
Anne Foster-Clarke

It had been cloudy and cold all day, but as the day turned into dusk on the night before Christmas Eve, the sky began to clear. The girl went to the back door and looked out into the still farmyard. Light from the outside security lamp shone onto her thick blonde curly hair and outlined her body heavy with the child she carried.

A young man came round the corner of the barn. She could hear the scrunch of his boots as frost began to form on the concrete. He came to her in the doorway and said with suppressed excitement.

'Get your coat on Maddie. I think it's started.'

She hung on to him whilst she stepped into her wellingtons and put on her duffle coat. He smiled down at her as she tried unsuccessfully to do up all the fastenings.

'Not much longer Johnny. Soon I'll be thin again.'

He smiled his brown-eyed smile. She took his hand and they walked across the yard towards the old Nissen hut where they stored the winter bedding.

As they passed by the stableyard Johnny's

mare whinnied as she heard their footsteps. Maddie felt in her pocket. Her fingers closed around an old paper roll of polos.

'Look what I've found. She'll not rest until I've given her one.'

The girl opened the gate and walked up to Moonlight's stable. Moonlight eyed the packet of polos greedily, her bright bay head and black forelock handsome in the darkening night. Maddie put a polo on the palm of her hand and offered it up to the soft velvety muzzle. The mare snuffled up the sweet and looked for more.

'Just one more,' Johnny said and looked over the stable door at the mare's belly. 'you know Maddie, I'm not sure if she's going to last another three weeks. I think that stallion of your brother's got to her earlier than we thought.'

'Oh,' said Maddie 'I don't think so. It's her second foal so she's bound to look bigger than when she had Cloud. Although she was early with him, wasn't she?'

Johnny looked worried. 'I'll look at her before we go to bed. Come on, we might have missed something.' He took her hand impatiently.

As they approached the building Johnny switched on his torch. The beam of light lit up the straw bales inside the hut. They were arranged in two rough squares, each containing a Large Black gilt pig. Inside the makeshift pens the straw was bright and thick. An infra red pig lamp hung from the beam above. One of the pigs was snuffling, grunting and making a nest, pushing the straw into a satisfying circle, the other lay stretched out on her side. Maddie leant over, stroked the pig's belly and gently ran her fingers over the engorged teats. She squeezed it. A small white milky blob formed on the end.

'Don't think it'll be long now, do you?' she whispered to Johnny as he sat down on one of the bales.

He reached out and made room for her to join him. She looked out of the hut and into the night sky. It was still a little cloudy. She was disappointed, she had hoped with the frost there would be stars tonight. A rustle in the straw caught her attention. Suddenly there was liquid, movement and a small thud in the straw as the first piglet, encased in its own perfect sac, entered the world.

'Just look, Maddie.' Johnny said, smiling 'This little pig is our future. The beginning of our herd. Isn't it exciting.'

She laughed and hugged him 'We'll call it the Walnuttree Herd of Large Blacks. We'll show at all the best shows and win lots of rosettes.'

Just then another little pig popped out. They both went into action then, cleaning the mucus from the piglets' airways and lifting them towards the row of waiting teats. The gilt shifted her weight carefully to accommodate her new family, then produced seven more piglets. The other young gilt, spurred on by the excitement next door, followed suit and gave birth to nine piglets of her own. Maddie and Johnny stayed another hour, saw that each piglet was feeding properly, the afterbirth delivered in entirety and the gilts content.

Maddie felt stiff and a little cold after sitting for so long. She took Johnny's proferred hand gratefully.

'Tea, that's what we need now and lots of honey. Oh, look Johnny.'she said excitedly as she looked up into the night sky, 'the stars have come out. Aren't they amazing! I think it's a good omen. They've come out to welcome the new piglets!'

Just then Maddie heard a thud followed by a whinny. She looked at Johnny.

'Did you hear that?'

He grabbed her hand as they ran from the Nissen hut to the stableyard. Johnny opened the door of the tackroom and turned on the stable lights. He opened the door of Moonlight's stable. She was down and her breathing was laboured. He knelt down beside her, his hands gently moving over her taut body. Johnny tried not to show his anxiety to Maddie.

He said, 'I think I'll give Jim a call. I don't like the look of her.'

Maddie smiled at him, 'I don't think my big brother will be very pleased with you, he's gone to a smart dinner party tonight.' Johnny grinned back at her.' Well, he shouldn't be a vet then, should he?'

Johnny took out his mobile phone, selected Jim's number and waited. No reply. He stood under the stable light and texted him. Two minutes later Jim's voice boomed out of the phone.

'What's the matter, has my sister gone into labour? Phone the hospital you idiot.' Johnny cut in and said 'No, Jim she's fine. It's Moonlight. She's down and I don't like the look of her. Will you come?'

Jim could hear the anxiety in Johnny's voice. He was suddenly deadly serious. 'I'll get my kit. Be there in twenty minutes.' The phone went dead.

Maddie said, 'I'll bring you a flask of tea out, then I'll go to bed. Shout if you need me Johnny. Don't forget he'll need hot water, towels and soap.'

'I know the drill, Maddie. You get some rest while you can. I'll call you if ....?' His voice faltered 'if I need you.'

Maddie made a flask of tea, took it out to the tackroom, briefly looked over the stable door at Moonlight and Johnny and returned to the house. If something bad was going to happen she didn't want to know. Not now that her own ordeal was imminent. She turned her face against the possibility of disaster or death.

Ten minutes later she heard Jim's car roar into the yard. She moved the curtain and saw him still in his dinner jacket opening the boot of his car. She watched as he picked up his kit and strode across the yard to Moonlight's stable, then she got into bed and turned on the radio. Maddie didn't listen to the D.J's voice or his music but it blocked out what was going on outside. She hid her head under the duvet and tried to sleep. An hour went by and she still couldn't sleep, so she got up, drew the curtains, and looked out into the yard. She stood there for sometime then looked at the clock. It was just before midnight. Maddie looked up into the night sky, at a cloud that was covering some of the stars and then she saw it. A really big star from the east and it was right above the stableyard. At that moment she saw Johnny run towards the house. He called to her. She opened the window and looked down fearing the worst.

'Maddie, come down quick. She's all right Maddie, she's all right.'

Maddie didn't wait to hear anymore. She

got down the stairs as quickly as she could, put on her wellies, flung her duffle coat over her pyjamas and nearly collided with Johnny by the back door. He grabbed her hand and they ran over to the stableyard. They reached Moonlight's stable. Johnny opened the door and there she was. A beautiful filly foal. Moonlight was shaky and trembling, but she was up and nuzzling her new and most precious possession.

Jim stood in the corner of the stable savouring the moment. His dress shirt and trousers were covered in blood, mucus and shavings. He looked completely exhausted, but he was smiling.

'Had a helluva job to get her out, sis. A leg back and I thought I wouldn't get it round. Dear old Moonlight gave it everything, didn't you girl. Can't understand why she's so early. Lovely filly. What are you going to call her?'

Maddie said, 'Look outside both of you. Look at the sky.'

The two men walked to the stable door, looked up and saw the star shining above the stable.

'We're going to call her Star.' She laughed, 'Our very own Christmas Star.'

BEYOND THE DOOR
Mike Moody

Mary stared at the closed door, tears streaming down her face while she sobbed uncontrollably. Instinct overtook her shock and she dashed to the door, opened it and ran out into the rain. Herbert was near the end of the street, about to turn onto the main road.

'Bert! Come back.' Her cry was ignored and she ran after him, but when she turned onto the main road he was nowhere to be seen.

'Herbert! Come back. Don't leave us.' She stood silent for a moment then the enormity of her loss hit her and she pulled on her hair, dropped onto her knees letting out a piercing scream. Drawn curtains twitched and opened. Faces appeared, looking out to see what was happening, but nobody came out to help her. The rain trickled down Mary's back and brought her back to reality. She raised her head and saw the open curtains and felt ashamed at her behaviour. She had acted on a tide of emotion, not thinking of her neighbours or her children. In the doorway door of her house she saw Arthur and Florence standing there in their nightwear, looking frightened and lost. She stood up and curtains closed as she walked back slowly towards her waiting children. What was she going to say to them? As she got near she saw their worried faces.

Florence, the eldest at six, spoke. 'Mummy, why were you crying? Where's daddy?'

'Inside children. Let's not stand in the doorway.' They did what they were told. Mary closed the door, but did not lock it, hoping that Bert would change his mind.

'Now then you two! You should be in bed.'

'We heard the shouting, mummy, and the door banging shut. So I came down to see what was the matter and Arthur followed me. You weren't there and daddy wasn't there so we looked out and saw you kneeling at the end of the street. Why were you kneeling? Were you praying?'

'Yes Florence, I was praying very hard.'

'Why, mummy?'

'I can't say now, but we'll have a talk tomorrow when you get back from school. Now take Arthur to bed and go straight to sleep. No messing.'

As usual Mary gave the children a kiss

before going upstairs to bed, but they just stood there.

Mary looked at them and raised her voice,'Upstairs! Now!'

Florence looked at her with surprise and Arthur's bottom lip curled. 'We haven't had a kiss from daddy.'

'Daddy's not here Florence, but I'll give you his kiss, then you go straight upstairs.'

She kissed them again and they rushed upstairs. Feeling abandoned and bewildered she sat down by the fire and stared at the door. *Why? Why? Bert, you never talked to me about being unhappy. I don't understand. I have our baby on the way, due in three months. You must come back. I haven't the money to pay the rent and feed the children. How could you do this to us?*

She started crying again, but made sure it was not loud enough for the children to hear. The hours went by as she stared at the clock, but Herbert did not come back and night turned to day. She had to deal with practicalities, it was time for Florence to get ready for school. Once Florence had left for school she would walk to the mill and see if Herbert was at work.

She called up to Florence to make sure she was awake and getting dressed. No sooner had she shouted than Florence was running down the stairs, dressed and wide awake.

'You're an early bird today. Don't run down the stairs. I don't want you falling down and breaking your neck.'

'Has daddy come back?'

'No dear. I've decided to go to the mill once you're at school and I'll find out if he's there. If he isn't then I must go and see your grandma. But I should be back before school finishes.'

Florence looked like she was on the verge of crying and Mary gave her a hug and talked gently to her, 'I'm sure everything will turn out alright. You just pay attention to your schoolwork and don't worry about anything. Put a smile back on that pretty face and go and sit at the table and I'll bring your porridge to you.'

The porridge was dished up and while Florence was eating Mary dashed upstairs to see if Arthur was awake. She walked into the bedroom and Arthur was fast asleep, not a worry in the world. She looked at him and saw the similarity to his father. Her eyes welled up but she shook her head and got on with things, giving Arthur a gentle push to wake him up. His eyes opened.

'Come on, big boy, I need you up and dressed.'

Arthur yawned. 'It's dark mummy.'

'Yes, I need you to get up a bit earlier today as I'll be taking you for a walk after Florence goes to school'

'Where to?'

'We'll go to daddy's workplace and then maybe to your gran's. You'll like that won't you?'

'Yes. I think so.'

'Right, start dressing and come downstairs when you're ready. But don't take long. If you have any trouble with your buttons leave them for me to fasten.'

Mary went downstairs and saw that Florence was just finishing her porridge.

'Hurry up with that porridge Florence and get your hair brushed.'

Florence ate the last few spoonfuls, then fetched her hair brush and started brushing, but her mind was elsewhere.

'Florence! You're making a right mess of

your hair. Do you want some help?'

'Please mum. I wish daddy was here.'

As Mary finished brushing, Arthur joined them, part dressed. Florence ran over and gave him a hug and a kiss.

'You be good while I'm at school and do what mummy tells you to do.'

Arthur nodded his head. 'Bye bye Flo.'

'See you later.'

Mary and Arthur stood at the back door waving to Florence until she went out of the back yard and disappeared behind the wall.

'Right young man let's get you sorted.' She fastened his shirt and trousers and once he had put his shoes on she tied his shoelaces.

'Now let's get your coat and scarf on, then we're off.'

Outside it was very cold with a sharp frost. Arthur held her hand tight to avoid slipping. The walk to the mill would only take twenty minutes by which time it would be nine and there was a good chance of seeing the gatekeeper. As they walked down the street Mary hoped she would not bump into any neighbours, but her hopes were shattered when Mrs Crabtree appeared.

''Morning Mary. What's been going on? There was a bit of commotion last night. Is everything alright?'

'Sorry I can't stop Mrs Crabtree. I must take Arthur to his grandma and we're running late. Maybe see you later.' Mary walked on at a quick pace.

They arrived at the factory gatehouse. Mary was pleased to see there were no haulage wagons lined up waiting to unload their bales of wool, so she was confident of seeing the gatekeeper. Sure enough he was in the gatehouse attending to some paperwork.

''Morning, Mr Shepherd. Is Herbert in work? He didn't come home last night.'

' 'e's not here lass. 'e's norm'ly on't dot.'

'Oh! I must go and see if his mum has seen him. I hope he's alright.'

'Aye. Best do that, luv. Hope 'e's got a good excuse.'

Mary walked away. She had told a lie and didn't feel good about it, but she couldn't tell Mr Shepherd that he had walked out on her. She looked down at Arthur and gave him a smile. He smiled back.

'We've got a long walk to your gran. But

you like seeing you gran don't you?'

'Yes mummy. Will I get a bun?'

'Maybe, if your gran baked yesterday.'

The walking was slow, what with her being pregnant and Arthur's little legs, so it took just over an hour to get to her mum's. As ever the house looked immaculate, the privet hedge in the small front yard clipped neatly, the gate painted a dark green, the paths and door as clean as can be.

She knocked on the door and waited. She heard running and the door opened and her sister Rosebelle was there with a big smile.

'Mary! How lovely to see you.' They kissed and Rosebelle gave Arthur a big hug and lifted him up. 'What a big little man you are. Come and see your Gran, she's in the kitchen.'

They walked through the hallway and went into the kitchen, where Mary's mum was doing some baking.

She turned and smiled at her daughter. 'Well, Mary, what are you doing here? Haven't you got enough work to do in your own house? Not that you should be doing too much in your condition. How's Bert?'

'Mum, I'd like to speak to you on your own.

Rosebelle will you take Arthur out and look after him while I have a chat with mum.'

'Course I will. Come on Arthur, sit down with me and I'll tell you a story.' Arthur smiled and happily left the room with Rosebelle.

Mary looked at her mum and tears welled in her eyes.

'What's the matter, love?'

'Mum, Bert's left me.'

'What!? Did you have a row about something?'

'No. He just said he might as well be living in hell and he was leaving. He said he loved us all and that you and Dad will look after us. He shut the door on us and I couldn't believe what he said. I expected him to come back, but when he didn't I ran after him. He must have heard me shouting but I couldn't find him. I thought I might catch him at work this morning but he didn't turn up. I don't know what to do.'

'Have you tried his mother, sisters or brothers? I know he had a fall out with his family when he married you, thinking he was too young to marry. But he might have gone back to them to talk it over. He is their flesh and blood. If you like I'll go see his Mum, it's only fifteen minutes' walk from here. You make yourself some tea and have a slice of cake. I won't be long.'

Her mum left and she had a look in on Rosebelle and Arthur. Her sister could always tell a good story and Arthur was absorbed in the world she was creating. It brought back times when Bert would read stories to Florence and Arthur before they went to bed. When he'd finished reading he would give them a kiss and tell them to give her a kiss and then go to bed. She had to get these thoughts out of her head and went back into the kitchen. However as she slowly had her tea and cake she felt lost, with one word on her mind, 'why'?

It wasn't long before her mum returned. Mary could see there was no good news.

'She was sympathetic, love, but she had no idea where Bert was. She'll ask her daughters and sons if they've heard anything, but it seems unlikely.'

'What do I do, mum? I'll have to pay the rent at the end of the week, but I've no money coming in.'

'There's only one thing you can do, come back home. We'll squeeze you and the children in somehow. Your dad's working and your younger brothers have all got good jobs. We've enough income to look after you. But it might be a bit of a squash. You and Florence can sleep in Rosebelle's room and Arthur can sleep with your brothers.'

'Thanks mum.' She was grateful and knew it was the only course to take, yet she was used to living with her husband and children. She had built her own home and now that was nothing and what of the new baby, coming into the world with no father? The future ahead felt overwhelming. How on earth would she cope?

***

Mary and the children settled in very well and there were no problems with the birth of her boy. It was decided that he would be called James after his grandfather. Once the birth was over, Mary's thoughts turned to the loss of her husband, all the time trying to understand what caused him to leave. Her mum saw that she had problems with her eating and sleeping and decided to talk to her.

'Mary, you need to eat more and look after

yourself, otherwise you'll not have the milk for James.'

'Don't worry Mum I'm eating ok. My problem's sleeping. I just can't get Bert out of my mind. I don't understand what he said to me before he left. I feel guilty, that I must have done something wrong and the children have suffered because of it. I feel that I'm not good enough to be their mother'

'Don't speak like that Mary. You've been a wonderful mum. Your children love you and you can't be blaming yourself for Bert walking out on you. He betrayed you and his children. He was a wicked man and if your father and uncles came across him he'd get more than a mouthful.'

'You're right Mum. I must think like that, but it's hard. The children love being here with you and Dad. He always has time to answer their questions and he plays with them when he can. I'll do my best to sleep better and try get Bert off my mind'

Time went on and James went on to solid foods, but Mary felt no better. Depression hung over her and now that James didn't need her milk she felt useless. One day she decided she had to do something to overcome her depression and help the family.

'Mum, would you mind feeding James in a morning while I try and get some sleep. I need to get out of this weary state that I've been in. Then I can try and get some work and contribute to the family income.'

'Of course I don't mind. I'd love to see you back to your old self and I think I've had enough practice in looking after babies. So don't you worry, Florence is doing well at school and helps around the house. Also Arthur will be starting school shortly and I think Ernest will be moving out soon. I feel wedding bells in the air.'

'That's great mum. If you don't mind I'll go upstairs and try and catch up with some sleep. I'm glad to hear about Ernest but I won't say anything until he makes it official.'

Mary went back to the bedroom and laid on the bed with some hope of getting to sleep. But she could not get the sleep she needed and despite her feeling of guilt for not looking after the children and not helping with the housework she stayed in bed.

The next day Mary's mum went into the

bedroom. 'Mary, you need to get out of that bed, get something to eat and put something back into your life.'

'Yes mum. But I'm so tired.'

'And so you will be as long as you stay in that bed feeling sorry for yourself. Florence and Arthur have been asking to see you but I can't let them see you like this. It would upset them.'

'I don't want them to see me like this. Tell them I'm ill and they can come in when I feel better.'

'But Mary you need to get up, eat and work.'

'Just give me another night.'

Her mum walked out and went downstairs. Mary made an effort to get out of bed and she managed to walk to her mother and father's bedroom. A wash bowl and mirror stood on a chest of drawers. Her father's razor was by the bowl. She took it along with a towel and went back to her bed.

Later that day her mum came to check her. She saw her daughter, eyes shut and her complexion as white as the sheet. Her arm hung over the side, a towel wrapped around it soaked in blood. Mary's mum touched her cheek and she was cold. She touched her lips and there was no breath. Then, the final horror, there was no heart beat.

'Oh Mary! No. Lord God, please bring her back!'

***

Florence and Arthur were told that their mother had died of a broken heart. The death certificate bore the same information, enabling her to be buried in consecrated ground.

THANK YOU
Judith Osborne

Anita's immediate horizon was limited to the shoulder height gorse bushes. Frosty, spangled, spiky, the visible route was a single width trodden snow track, a hundred metres ahead to the next bend and two hundred metres back to the last one. A very slight upward slope would present a mild undulation of terrain. Good! Phone out ready for a quick photo memento at the top.

The ear-slicing gull squawk right overhead made her jump and look up. Out of the corner of her eye she saw a young girl pounding up behind her, away from her granny, with a springer spaniel, all legs and ears, ahead of her, then wham! The dog had shifted direction ever so slightly and the child tumbled across it, flat on her face with a yell of fear, outrage and quite possibly, pain.

Granny shouted, 'Coming, dear, coming!' as she quickened pace to the best of her ability. She looks somehow familiar, 'Where might I know her from?' thought Anita.

She and Granny reached the sobbing child almost simultaneously, and both peered down at a bleeding nose and chin. Anita hauled out a couple of tissues from her pocket, called Jasmine her retriever and bent to start the mop up operation.

'That was a nasty wallop, dear. Can you manage to get up if I help you? It'll make it easier to mop you clean. And dry the slush off you, come to that!'

'I'm sorry, she might not understand you. She only arrived in the country last week' Granny said. She looked uncomfortable and almost guilty as she spoke.

'Ah, that makes a nasty fall even worse, doesn't it, when you think nobody will know how you feel or what you want? Where does she live, then?'

'Oh, she'll be living here now. You OK, darling?' Granny smiled into the girl's face, questioning and loving simultaneously.

'I OK', the girl answered and pushed their springer away from her tear and bloodstained face. 'Want up.'

The two women helped her to her feet. Anita's careful dabs cleaned the child's face, then they looked at each other over her head. In that instant Anita knew where she had seen the other woman, 'Oh, hello! Well, this is a better place to meet than the hospital, isn't it? I've only just realised where I saw you. How are you? Can I do anything more to help? I have my car if you need a lift home, or, er, back to school? Oh, you've only just arrived here, so I presume you're not at a school yet.' Anita smiled at the child, then at Granny, whose face was tense. Waiting for a response, and trying to work out what was best to do next, Anita bent down again to encourage both dogs to give their own version of sympathetic attention to the child, but with one restraining hand planted on each chest. Their wagging tails and long pink tongues caught the girl's eye and her sobs became gulps and hiccups.

'Oh, yes. The scan day a couple of weeks ago. I'm better. Better.' said Granny, 'I've got to go back, though. I'm bracing myself. How about you?'

'Well ditto, but I think I'm in the clear. I've already had one op. and my surgeon says she's happy.'

'I'm so glad to hear that. You've been a

great help, dear, and Karina and I are more than grateful.'

'You good lady,' Karina broke in 'I like you.'

'I'm Audrey, and Karina and I both say thank you very much. Karina?'

'Thank you very much.'

'Just for simplicity shall I call you 'Granny'?' asked Anita, 'and I'm actually 'Granny' as well, but please – Anita! Then on an impulse she added, 'Well, I vote we go to the burger van that I spotted in the car park. Even the dogs can share the end of a burger. Or do you like hot dogs, Karina?'

'Um, she probably hasn't had many, but yes, I think that would go down well. I could enjoy one myself. In the absence of alcohol. Sorry, I do confess I've had a particularly bad few weeks.' A tentative smile accompanied these words. Anita, immediately assuming health issues above all, hoped she was removing any surprise from her own expression as she replied,

'A drop of alcohol can be a useful ally, yes,' and Audrey had not actually answered her question about Karina. Had she after all let herself in for a fair size drama?

There was the distraction of the two dogs, the promise of the treat clarified, plus Anita's running commentary on the winter conditions, the gorse bushes, sky clouds and seagulls, not to mention some distant hikers. The return to the car park seemed almost pain free for Karina.

'Hurt here, and here' was heard a few times, a finger pointing at her own face and her left knee, but a gentle pat, and a murmured 'Oh dear, soon be better,' seemed sufficient response to keep the child moving forward reasonably happily. Single file progress prevented general chat.

'The little lady looks as if she needs a present. Please have this,' said the young man at the burger stall, hot dog in hand to offer to a wide – eyed Karina, who did a few little jumps, a beam now across her face.

The burger and hot dog consumption was completed with vocal satisfaction all round. 'Oh, lovely, lovely,' and 'Just what the doctor ordered for injured people!' Karina had wolfed large chunks of hers, then tried to push almost half into Jasmine's open jaws, their springer jumping up and down the while. 'Thank heaven for placid dogs!'

Granny's car was identified, Karina pointed a confident finger, with another beam of pleasure. In theory only farewells remained to be formulated, and yet Anita hesitated. There was something she was missing, some vital fact that would turn this chance encounter into a significant meeting, she was sure. By nature empathetic, but reticent, and reluctant to show the kind of interest in other people's affairs that could be construed as 'nosiness', she would not allow herself to formulate the direct questions that hovered around the inside of her mouth, clamouring to be asked aloud. Was this 'Granny', who seemed so close to the little girl, actually Granny? If so was she 'in charge' of Karina permanently or only temporarily? If permanently, where was the child's mother? Father, come to that? And very importantly, where had Karina come from, with her accented, limited English? Surely that was a question she could ask without instigating a fatal avalanche of information or emotions that would engulf them all?

'So has Karina come from very far away?'

she heard herself ask in rather too bright a tone. Sure enough, Audrey's face no longer smiled.

'Well, that's been part of the difficult few weeks I mentioned. I'd like to tell you. I just don't want to get you involved in my problems; it wouldn't be fair at all.'

'Give me a few broad brush strokes, perhaps – I must admit I'm interested, and I would help if you needed it and thought I could.'

'That's so kind. But, you know, wouldn't it be better if we spoke over a hot cup of coffee? Are you in a hurry, or would you like to follow me – I'm only ten minutes or so away by car?'

'I'll do that, thank you. Lead on!'

The sky was beginning to darken with increasing cloud, a few lights were on, and the temperature was dropping as the two cars shunted around to park in the driveway of an Edwardian house near a minute triangle of park, called 'Maids' Park', Anita registered in passing. She clutched her ancient jacket close around her neck as questions about the outcome of this random encounter flitted through her brain.

'I help,' was Karina's first happy offer,

accepted with her Granny's usual warm smile and loving thanks.

The wintry garden gave promise of future delights. The house was calm and inviting. Anita felt alert for clues as to the 'something significant' that she was certain was still to come of this.

'This is wonderful coffee, thank you, and I know Karina helped.'

'Put bikkits,' Karina managed.

'Yes, you chose them from the cupboard and arranged them on the plate – so helpful! Right, and of course the coffee machine helped, too – it's a major gift from Simon, Uncle Simon, out of all proportion to my modest kitchen, but welcome, very welcome!' The tension in Granny's face had returned and her coffee mug was in a tight grip.

'Was it a birthday present, then?' asked Anita, 'obviously an inspired idea, anyway.'

Granny took a deep gulp of breath, 'This child has been on the move in very difficult circumstances for too long and I need to help.' Her eyes filled with immediate tears, 'Oh, dear, I must try. Oh, thank you, darling!' as Karina clambered to kneel on the sofa and wind her arms around Granny's neck.

'No cry, please, no cry, no sad. Happy. Karina happy, you happy. This home. Good home, good Granny, good lady,' as she twisted her head round to bless Anita with yet another firm smile.

Granny was plainly finding it difficult to continue her story, and Anita, no longer comfortable, shifted uneasily in her chair. This was starting to look like just the territory she did not want to be in; very 'personal', and possibly complicated. And most likely 'none of her business'. But Granny was speaking again, hesitantly, slowly, in not much more than a murmur, close to Karina's dark hair, 'Simon is an honorary Uncle and the Prince of Uncles, I can tell you. He's a volunteer in one of the camp schools on the Turkish border. Karina was there for a while.'

'Uncle Simon good,' came Karina's voice.

Anita's brain felt distinctly fuzzy; Ok, what camp? Which Turkish border? This had to be a refugee drama.

'This young lady first of all made the journey from Mosul to the big refugee camp next to the border in Turkey, then after six months she was brought the rest of the way. Everything masterminded by Simon. Which is all good – Karina even went to school, and the arrangements were kind and the best anyone could have done. But the background – much emptiness - '

'Yes, oh I do see what you mean, oh yes. A lot has maybe been, sort of misplaced, maybe even lost along the way?'

'Exactly that. And who knows when or how such items can be found or replaced? I'll just say 'maternal and paternal relatives' and you'll know straight away how traumatic the situation is. Plus not all the necessary paperwork is in its proper place here,' she sighed heavily, 'and I have no means of helping to supply that. Karina, my love, where is your book? Please find it. Upstairs, I think. Off you go'.

The child unravelled herself, slid off the sofa and trotted out of the room.

'Yes, well, he went out to teach in one of the two schools they have. It's a much better set up than you might expect. In fact the Syrians who are there mostly don't want to come into England, they are so grateful to the Turks for their kindness.

'But Karina isn't Syrian, is she? It's a Greek name, I thought.'

'No, you're right, her father is my nephew and he married a Greek girl,' she stopped, gulped, and almost wailed her next words, 'He stopped sending me emails, I wondered what on earth was wrong. We'd always been in contact. Then his wife sent a message to say she was out of her mind with worry and would I go and see her. When I did, she told me he had been radicalised. Heaven knows how. She thought it was online brainwashing. I had no idea, no idea that such a thing was possible and neither did she. But that's how he came to be in Mosul – fighting on the wrong side,' she broke down again, 'and now he's most likely dead, and his wife. She followed him out there and only told me once she was on the way over there. Said she just had to go and find him, taking Karina with her. Unbelievable. Truly unbelievable. Also brainwashed, I suppose, in a different way. It's such chaos out there, there's no means of checking for sure what's happened to them. Simon hopes he can find out – he's my neighbour's son, actually. But this lovely little girl, what's going to happen to her?'

'Oh dear, how absolutely hideous all round. I so understand why you're in such a state. And I do take it you're', she hesitated, 'on your own?'

'Yes, but I sort of always have been, from choice. I've enjoyed my independence, and always been well supported. And I've had the pleasure of the daily company of small children as a nursery teacher. But this is in a different category, a lot more demanding than anything I've faced yet.'

'Well don't despair. I do believe I may actually be able to help, as I hoped – although I didn't realise the nature of your difficulty. Are you in contact with Simon? By phone, for instance?' As Audrey nodded bemusedly, Anita allowed herself the beginnings of a smile, 'you see, unlikely as the coincidence may seem, my own son, Michael, is rather closely involved with one of the major charities working out there, as a co-ordinator. If we can establish some details of the couple and their last known whereabouts, through Simon's information, he may just be able to move this a step or two further forward. Plus the charity might be persuaded to be in contact with you in a constructive way. Would that be OK as a plan at least? What I can't sort out for you is all the forms you need to fill in and the interviews you'll have to have to make things acceptable to the authorities, and I mustn't claim Michael can do much on that, either.'

With the fourth attempt two days later she was able to get hold of Michael by phone. He listened almost without comment to her story, and came on board with the plan,

'I won't say 'no problem', Mum, but I'll give it my best shot.' She arranged top up money for his mobile and then firmly backed off to let him get on with whatever he could set up. With sinking heart she could hear the allied bomb attacks while she was struggling to speak to him on a defective line. Better just not to think about that. He had tried to reassure her. He had then done what he could to help, and was now on the way home. 'On the way' was how Anita had to cope with her extreme concern about him, but at least home really did mean her home for a few days.

The day the doorbell rang and it was Michael, with a smile on his face, was almost unbearable in its emotion.

Two weeks later, the week before Christmas, heavy greyness prevailed again, even the slush had disappeared, and not a handkerchief of blue sky showed. Anita was back in the same chair at Audrey's. Karina stood neatly on the hearth rug, with a tentative smile for the guest. The big box of chocolates rather tightly clutched in her hands was slowly transferred to Anita, who expressed due appreciation and instantly ripped it open,

'There you are, dear, choose one for each of us, please!'

Audrey was full of anticipation, 'I can't believe I can almost look forward to Christmas. Your son has been another honorary Uncle for us – he's been just wonderful. You are so lucky, but then, so is he to have you as his mother. Of course not everything is as we would want it, and the paperwork we still have to do is a total nightmare in my life, but so much is clearer, so much is better than I dared to hope. You know that Michael spoke directly to a volunteer on the outskirts of Mosul who knew Karina's mother. He reached her, and told her he could put Michael's mobile directly into her hands?' she tried not to sob, 'so Karina spoke to her

Mummy yesterday on the phone, although (clearing her throat) her Daddy is not well enough. That was such a treat, wasn't it, darling?'

'Mummy here soon? Want Mummy here soon.'

'Yes, well we don't yet know exactly when you'll see her, but in the meantime Father Christmas will come and bring you presents, for sure, and some of them will definitely be from Mummy.'

'And Daddy?'

'Yes, and Daddy; we'll make sure of that,' Audrey's voice was almost steady.

'I'm so relieved and glad Michael was able to help. I have the huge treat that he's coming to me at Christmas with his wife and their new daughter. He missed her birth, and we've all been missing him so desperately that I shall be spoiling him, and them, out of all proportion! It would be such fun if we could all meet up – shall we?'

Anita allowed herself a laugh of delight. From the hearthrug,

'Yes, yes! Good lady, nice lady! Thank you! Thank you!'

A Perfect Christmas
Joan Roberts

Oct:

Christmas shopping in October to avoid the annual rush

Nov

All the baking in November, an extra freezer saves a crush

Dec

Order Turkey early, wrap your presents and trim your tree

Prepare your meals the day before so your Christmas day is free.

***

Evie read the poem scribbled in the back of an old diary of her mother's and smiled. Nearly every Christmas that she could remember had been chaotic, last minute catastrophes, baking failures and burnt offerings. There was the Christmas when the turkey wouldn't fit in the oven and had to be sliced and fried as Mum tried desperately to keep the veg warm. The year of the electricity cut that was celebrated with cheese sandwiches, *thank goodness we bought all those candle*s. Somehow though they had been able to laugh about it all, and then there was last year. Evie sat back on her ankles. Last year when Mum lost her balance bringing the shopping up the stairs because the lift was out of order again, and she fell backwards down the whole of the last flight, breaking two ribs and her left leg. She had lain there for two hours until Mrs. Jackson from number 30 had found her.

'I called the ambulance, but you know what it's like,' she explained later. 'It took ages to come, the traffic being so bad this time of year.' Evie knew only too well. It had taken her a long time to get to the hospital from work when they called, by which time her mother had developed pneumonia from the shock of the fall. Maureen, who had met her at the hospital, was adamant.

'We'll have to cancel Christmas altogether, if Mum's not there we shouldn't do it at all.'

'What about your kids, Mo? You can't

cancel their Christmas. Mum would hate that.'

'Well no, not for them. We'll let them open their presents and do their stockings, but we won't be able to celebrate the way we usually do. Mum may not get out until well after Christmas. Perhaps we'll have a coming home party instead.' Evie knew that Mo didn't want to say what they were both thinking.

In fact they had taken a few things to the hospital on Christmas day. Effie, Mo's five year old, had made a little Christmas tree and decorations. They all took crackers and whatever they'd made or bought for Mum, but she wasn't even well enough to drink a cup of tea. It had been the worst Christmas ever. When they got back to Mo's, who had insisted that Evie stay with her over the holiday, neither of them felt like celebrating. They played a few games with the children, put them to bed and watched Reg drink his Guinness. They couldn't even enjoy Christmas Day 'Strictly'. There had never been a time that either could remember being in bed before midnight on Christmas day.

Evie sighed as she looked at the picture of her mum with Effie when she was born, with little Mark at their side pointing to his new baby sister. It was from Mark and Mum that Effie got her name. Mo had wanted to call her Ffion and had written the name down for Mum who questioned the spelling.

'There are too many Fs,' she'd said.

'She's Effie,' Mark said.

Evie put the photo with her keepsakes and stretched. Around her all her memories packed up in large plastic sacks and old cardboard boxes standing ready just as she was to move on. Just then the doorbell rang and made her jump. She had to move a few of the black plastic bags to the side of the room.

'That blooming lift is only out of order again,' panted Mo. 'How's it going, you nearly done? I do hope so. I've no energy left after all those stairs.'

'Is Reg coming up or is he waiting in the car?'

'How much of all this are you taking?' Mo looked around at the boxes and black sacks lining the living room and moved into the kitchen. 'Reg is with the kids in the car. Do you need his help, only we haven't picked up the turkey yet? We're going past the Co-op on the way home; it was too crowded when we set off.'

'And you think it will be less crowded on the way back?' Evie looked at her sister and suddenly realised just how much like their mother she was. She walked over and gave her a hug. 'I've paid someone to clear all this after Christmas, the place doesn't have to be empty until the fifteenth of January. Thank goodness for Christmas, otherwise we'd be in a real state. I wouldn't fancy dragging all this downstairs.' She showed Mo the poem in the back of the diary. Mo put her arm around Evie's shoulders and kissed her cheek as they shared a minute of quiet reflection on the events of the last year.

Picking up the box of keepsakes they headed for the door.

'I'll just take a last look round in case,' said Mo as she wiped her eyes on her sleeve. Evie waited outside at the top of the stairs trying hard not to feel too miserable. After all it would be Christmas again in a few days and she felt they both owed it to the children and good old Reg to make the very best of things this year.

They joined with the children singing carols in the car, even Reg, although Effie complained that he made her 'sing wrong.' They finally managed to get a parking space to do the last of the shopping.

'Who wants to help with the tree when we get home?' Reg said, mainly to Effie.

'I want to put the fairy on the top', she said.

'Why does it have to be a fairy?' asked Mark. 'Why can't it be Spiderman?' Mark had been a Superman fan since he was three but now at nearly eight he had changed his allegiance since their visit to the latest Spiderman film during the holidays.

'Haven't you decorated the tree yet? I have it on good authority that it should be done early in December.' Evie put her arm around Mark. 'A fairy brings good luck, or that's what we hope.' She looked down on the turkey which was defrosting into her lap and hoped that it wouldn't be too big for Mo's oven.

When they got to the house Mo led them all into the front room so that they could get going on the tree while she put the shopping away.

'Mum, what on earth are you doing?' Evie couldn't believe her eyes as she saw her mother standing on a stool putting the finishing touches to the top branches of the tree. Reg walked across and helped her down. 'After all you've been through with that leg of yours this year how could you start climbing around?'

'Oh don't fuss, I'm so excited about Christmas this year and I wanted to be finished by the time you got here.'

'I should send you straight to your room for being disobedient, you daft old woman.' Mo went over to her mother and hugged her tight before leading her to her Christmas present, a reclining armchair.

'Can I put the fairy on now?' said Effie.

'Oh wait,' said Evie and ran to the hall. When she came back she passed something to Effie. Reg picked Effie up and she placed the figure on the pinnacle of the tree. Mo had already opened a bottle of champagne and filled four glasses, Mark handed Effie a glass of milk, and he had blackcurrant squash in his Spiderman cup.

'Oh Evie, our old fairy, I thought it was broken', said Mum. Just then something fell from the fairy and landed on the floor. There was a flash and the tree lights went out while the remainder of the fairy hung by one foot and eventually fell through the tree. Evie picked it up.

'I thought it might bring us good luck,' she said.

Reg fixed the lights. Then he produced a bit of fuse wire from his workbox and whispered something to Mark, who ran upstairs with an enormous grin on his face. When he returned Reg lifted him up and Mark fixed his Spiderman figure firmly to the top of the tree.

'Well that's something we haven't done before,' said Mum. They all raised their glasses.

'To Spiderman, for saving the day and a perfect Christmas, as it always is when we're all together.'

The Gift
Nikki McDonagh

Dan sang along to the tune on the radio. It was a well-known Christmas track that brought back memories of family gatherings with dry turkey, boozy cakes, and sticky glasses of eggnog. He pulled the tinsel garland from his neck and wound it round the large steering wheel.

The smell of pine from the Norwegian Spruce that lay across the backseat made his nose itch. He drove fast, wanting to get home before his wife so that he could hide the car in the garage. He'd bought a massive tarpaulin to drape over it, and a big red ribbon tied in a bow to stick on top. She was going to love it.

So what if it did cost a small fortune to have the classic 1953 green Cadillac converted from automatic to manual, Karen was worth it. Besides, it was a two-way gift. A Christmas present and a peace offering to say sorry for that silly little affair with Janice. Christ, it didn't mean anything. It was just a simple dalliance, you know, a fifty something male menopausal hiccup.

Office parties, especially around that time of year, were dangerous places for the long term married. But he felt bad all the same. Especially when he saw the look on Karen's face after Janice told her; it almost stopped his heart. Dan's throat clenched and he swallowed.

He breathed in the chilly air, then smiled as he looked out of the windscreen onto the shiny bonnet.

Yes, this car would make up for it. Just like the diamond 'forever ring' he bought Karen five years earlier when he couldn't be held responsible for the meaningless fling that was just a one-night-stand, with Laura, the neighbours' foreign exchange student.

Wasn't his fault she liked her men craggy and slightly pot-bellied. She went back to France after three months and the thing ended. Karen forgave him, again, all sorted.

A song with sleigh bells, nasal singing, and flutes distracted him from his guilt, but not the wobble that began under the brake pedal.

At first, it was nothing more than a slight juddering under his right foot. Dan released the pressure on the accelerator and the vibration stopped. He shuffled in his seat and the radio went dead. He twiddled with the dials, but the only sounds that came out were crackles and buzzes that hurt his ears, so he turned it off. An echo of static fizzed from the speakers. It became loud and shrill, like a woman shrieking. Dan peered out of the windscreen, half expecting to see someone in the middle of the road yelling, but all he saw were high hedges and a long narrow road without streetlights or cat's eyes.

A low mist rose as the sun sank below the horizon. Ice filled ditches reflected the darkening sky making it look like a heavenly oil spill. Dan watched rabbits slip on the frozen water as they made their way to the fields beyond the leafless wall of bramble and hedgerow. He looked at his wristwatch and tutted. It was getting late, growing darker by the second and he hated driving at night.

He shifted gear and pressed down on the accelerator. The car lurched, made a high whining sound and swerved to the left. Dan yanked on the steering wheel and slammed on the breaks. The engine died and he came to a stuttering halt in the middle of the road.

'Oh great, just what I need.' He slapped the steering wheel with both palms, then sat back and pulled out his mobile phone. No reception. With a sigh, he opened the car door and stepped out into the gloom. The air was still and cold. All was silent except for the raspy cry of a nearby pheasant. He rubbed his hands together, stamped his feet on the frosty ground and sat on the warm bonnet of the car.

'Come on,' he said and tried his phone again. 'Finally.' He tapped in the number for a recovery vehicle and waited for an answer. 'Hi, yeah, I'm broken down on some little road just outside of Framlingham. Not sure. Wait a minute. Okay, I see a sign for Hoo Wood and a reindeer-petting event. Oh, and a Santa mobile ride a mile ahead. North, I think. Yeah, I did pass that. Okay, great. What? Two hours? But…okay, two hours.'

The light began to fade rapidly as steel-grey clouds billowed in, threatening snow. The phone vibrated and chimed. 'Hi, Karen. Yeah, I know I said I'd be home before four, but…no, I am not with Janice. I am not. Call her if you don't believe me. We are not in cahoots. I told you it is over. Christ, it never was, anything.

She means nothing to me. Yes, exactly like Laura and Chrissie, which was fifteen years ago. Good grief, you're not going to drag that out again. I was never going to leave you for her. I don't know why she told you that. She was just a...yeah, yeah, like all the rest. What next time? Do you have to be so dramatic? Oh, charming. Well, the same to you. No, Karen, I didn't mean...'

The phone went dead. Dan winced, pulled his duffle coat around his shivering body, and climbed back into the Cadillac sedan. 'Why won't she believe me? Why don't you believe me?' he said into the redundant mobile phone and stuffed it into his inside coat pocket.

Dan sat and waited. The warmth inside changed to a biting cold. He blew on his hands and rubbed his shins, but it was no good, the chill burrowed into his flesh and gnawed at his bones. 'This is ridiculous,' he shouted and pressed his head against the steering wheel. Tinsel tickled his flesh and he ripped the decoration away.

He put his forehead against the wheel and let it sink into the stiff leather. The veins in his temples pulsed against it and for a moment, he felt the hide on the rim move in the same rhythmic beat. He raised his head, glared down at the black stitching and saw it twitch. 'Nah. No, this is stupid.' He fumbled for the door handle and pushed down. It opened with a creak and Dan got out quickly.

His skin prickled and he shook himself to dispel the feeling of weird that blew over him like a bitter wind. He smacked his lips, delved into his coat pocket and pulled out his mobile. His fingers shook as he punched in the number of the classic car sales room. *In the Bleak Mid-Winter,* played for a few seconds, followed by a cheery voice wishing everyone, 'A very, Merry Christmas.'

'Great, you're still there. Look I've broken down and …' a recorded message told him that everyone had gone home for the holiday and hoped that he had a wonderful New Year. 'What? No, no, no, this is not happening!' He flung his phone onto the floor. The back flew off as it bounced on the cracked tarmac. Dan closed his eyes.

The temperature dropped. Something shrieked behind him. He reassured himself that the sound came from an owl. After all, there are plenty of them in the countryside. Dan raised his lids and blinked. His breath floated before his eyes in a hazy white cloud. A hollow ache formed in his belly. He breathed heavily and became dizzy. A missed lunch in favour of picking up the car, butterflies of expectations, and the quick swig of sherry the salesman gave him, was beginning to have an unwelcome effect on his digestion.

He pressed his hands on the hood of the car and let out a dry heave. A faint murmur drifted towards him and Dan thought he heard a voice in the distance. A curious feeling came over him. A longing; a wish for something that he knew he could never have.

Glancing down, he fixed his gaze on the silver figure perched at the edge of the bonnet. It was an odd thing, part woman part aeroplane, very streamlined, very evocative. Dan leaned closer as the moon, peaking through the heavy clouds, highlighted its slender shape.

In the shimmering glow, it seemed to move ever so slightly, as if stretching. Dan rubbed his face and took a deep breath. He bent lower and touched the female face with the tip of his finger. It vibrated.

'Dear god!' He withdrew his hand quickly and backed away. His head swam and his ears rang with a high-pitched buzz that caused him to lose his balance. He leant against the car door and the ringing stopped.

'They're not coming.'

Dan spun around and saw a platinum blonde haired woman walking towards him. She was small and thin, and wore a powder blue figure hugging evening gown. On her head was a filigree tiara, and attached to her shoulders were small white wings. She smiled then coughed. 'You got a cigarette?'

'No, sorry I don't smoke.'

The woman rolled her eyes, walked over to the Cadillac sedan and ran her fingers along the smooth hood emblem. 'Woman in flight,' she said.

'Sorry, what?'

'That's what she's called. The mascot.'

'Really? I never knew that.' Unnerved by her sallow complexion and vacant stare, he asked, 'Sorry, but, how did you get here?'

The woman winked and tapped her nose. 'Oh, that would be telling.' She touched the silver mascot and her face darkened. 'A fitting epithet don't you think?'

'I'm sorry I don't know what you mean.'

'You will.' She gave Dan a huge smile. 'It's my birthday today.'

'Happy birthday.'

'Why thank you. My name is Loretta. Actually, that's a lie, it's really Carol, but I hate the name, such a cliché. Just because I was born on Christmas Eve, doesn't mean I have to be named after the stupid holiday, does it?' She moved towards Dan, stood in front of him, tilted her head to one side, put her left hand on her hip and straightened. 'I think Loretta is far more sophisticated. Do you agree?'

'Erm, yeah, I suppose.'

Loretta smiled and stared into his eyes. Dan could not look away and became transfixed by the blackness of her pupils. He felt her touch his arm and move her hand underneath his coat sleeve. He shivered at the coldness of her fingers on his flesh and moved out of reach.

'Don't be like that. I'll think you don't like me. Where's your holiday spirit?'

'Miss, I don't know you, or how you got here, but I would very much prefer it if you just stayed where you are.'

'Party pooper,' Loretta said and pouted. She folded her arms and turned from Dan. 'Some men would die to have me pay them attention.'

Tightness gripped his throat and he gulped. Clouds rolled across the moon and all became black. He plunged his hand into his coat pocket, pulled out a tiny torch, and shone it down the empty tree-lined road. 'I don't know where the breakdown truck has gotten to? They should have been here by now.'

'They're not coming.'

He turned back to Loretta. 'What? How do you know?'

Loretta giggled and wiggled her way towards him. 'Aren't you going to sing *Happy Birthday to You*, to little old me?' She sat on the bonnet of the car and crossed her legs. 'No? Okay then, how about something more Christmassy? Nah. I'm not that cheesy.' Loretta pouted and tapped a rhythm onto the hood. She hummed a tune that Dan was vaguely familiar with, and began to sing *Your Cheatn' Heart,* by Hank Williams.

Dan opened his mouth to tell her to stop, but he didn't. Instead, he joined in, taking over when she stopped. On he sang until his mouth dried and his throat seized up. He touched his throat and coughed.

'You have a beautiful voice, Dan. Are you a professional singer?'

'Me? No. I don't usually sing at all.'

'Well, you should. I'd listen to you all day, Dan, I really would.'

'Wait a minute, how do you know my name?'

'You told me silly. Are you sure you don't have a cigarette?'

He shook his head and when Loretta sighed and jumped off the car, he twitched as if someone was shoving something sharp up his behind. She sashayed over, held out her arms and began to dance. 'Come on grab a hold. It will warm you up.'

Dan put his hands behind his back and Loretta giggled. 'My, my, aren't we the shy type. Come on Dan, one little dance. I'm not going to bite,' she said, and snapped her teeth shut. It sounded like bones clacking together. Dan's stomach clenched. He looked over his shoulder in the hope that someone was coming, but saw no one.

'Hey, Dannio, come on and give Loretta a

great big hug. No? Well then, let's just sway to the beat,' she said and sang, *That's Amore*, swinging her hips and moving closer to where Dan stood next to the green sedan. 'When the...' She winked and continued to hum the tune, raising her voice as she walked slowly towards him.

He stepped back. 'Look, Miss.'

'Loretta. Don't be so formal, Dannio.'

'Right, okay. Look, Loretta, I'm sorry, but I really don't think this kind of behaviour is appropriate.'

Loretta stopped moving. An expression of revulsion spread across her face. She folded her arms and stared at him. 'I swear, all you men are the same. Oh, it's fine when you want it, but if a girl takes the initiative, you clam up like a frightened little virgin. I'm beginning to wonder if you're worth the effort.' She stuck her chin out and gave Dan a narrow-eyed stare.

He sighed, turned and shone his torch down the road. 'The breakdown truck will be here soon. I'm sure of it. Then we can both get a lift back to civilisation.'

'Don't be silly.'

'What?'

'I told you before, they're not coming.'

Dan moved towards her, holding the torch in front of him.

Loretta held her hand in front of her mouth and stifled a snicker. 'The driver of the truck didn't see me. He was going too fast. When I waved to him, he swerved and crashed. Only had himself to blame really.'

'Dear god. Where did this happen?'

'Oh, a couple of miles down the road.'

'Did you call an ambulance?'

Loretta held her hands out, palms up and shrugged. 'I didn't see a telephone box.'

'Don't you have a mobile?'

'What's a mobile?'

'A mobile phone.'

'Now, you're teasing me. Telephones that move? For real? Kind of thing Lester would have said to rile me up. Before he lost the tenderness. He used to hang up a big old woollen stocking on Christmas Eve. Such a softie really. Well, in the beginning.'

Dan took a step back, shone the light around and saw where his phone lay by the front wheel of the car. He reached down for it, but before he could pick it up, Loretta placed her high-heeled foot upon it. She wagged a finger at him and said, 'Naughty boy. Today is my day, you have to give me all your attention.' Then she ground her heel into the phone and kicked the remains into the ditch. 'There, now no one can bother us.'

'Look, Miss…'

'Loretta! Say my name, Dan.'

'Okay, keep calm, Loretta.'

'I am calm. Always. Even when the punches came and the kicks and the slaps and the…' she trailed off and flicked her hair from her face. 'Oh, let's not talk of such nasty things. Hey, look.' She tilted her head upwards and looked to the sky. Small flakes of snow landed on her lips, and remained there un-melted. She licked them off and smiled. 'See, it's snowin'. Wouldn't be a proper Christmas without the white stuff, eh? White, and bright, and bright, and white. Just like the wedding dress I wanted. White, and bright, and bright, and white,' she sing-sang the words and twirled around. The wings on her back quivered like frightened mouse ears. Dan frowned and squeezed his eyes tight. Loretta increased her volume until she shouted the words, 'White, bright, bright, white.'

'For Christ's sake, stop it. What the hell are you rambling on about woman?'

'Don't "woman" me.' She stopped, glared at Dan and spoke in a hoarse whisper, 'That's what he called me when I annoyed him. You don't get the right to be so familiar, you, sap.' Loretta closed her mouth, smoothed her hair and pushed it behind her ears. 'I forgive you. I forgave Lester too.' She stared at the car and side grinned. 'Who ya got in the back?'

'No one.'

'Oh really? Then who is that lying there all stretched out?'

'That's not a "who" that's a "what". Look, it's a Christmas tree.'

'So, you've not been crawling around in the back, smoochin' with some floozy, then?'

'No. I've only just bought it.'

Loretta laughed. 'Boob.'

'I beg your pardon?'

'You bought a crash car. My, my, they saw you coming.'

Dan shone the light at the Cadillac. In the beam, the car looked different - shinier and brighter than he remembered. Loretta strutted over to him and fondled his fingers. She stared into his eyes and he let her take the torch from him. He watched as she used it to illuminate the backseat. He blinked as the fir transformed into two figures kissing. Loretta moved closer and as she did, the couple stopped their amorous canoodling and stared out of the window.

'I caught him red-handed, and on my birthday too. I thought he was going to propose. He said he had something to tell me, something festive. Silly me eh?' Loretta turned the torch on and off repeatedly. 'You married?'

'Yes.' Dan squinted when Loretta shone the light into his eyes. 'What was all that in the back seat? I thought I saw two people, but that's stupid, I mean, how did they get there and now they're gone and. Oh, I don't understand?' She dazzled him again. 'Stop that.'

'Baby. You don't look married,' Loretta said and swirled the torch around, blinding Dan. 'You know what?'

'What?'

'I lied about the truck.' She lowered the torch. 'Sorry.'

'It hasn't crashed?'

'Nah.' She held the light under her chin and opened her mouth wide like a tunnel. Then she said in exaggerated tones, 'I swallowed it, see?' Loretta moved closer to Dan, her lips stretched across her teeth. He saw blood on her tongue and gashes appeared on her cheeks and forehead.

'Christ! Who are you?'

Loretta turned off the light. She became a silhouette in the darkness and Dan backed away from her advancing steps. He bumped into the car and felt it shudder as the engine came to life briefly, then died. 'Christ!'

'Well, I'm not the saviour, that's for sure. Oh, now Hun, don't look so scared. Are you frightened of me?' Dan nodded. 'But I'm just a girl. I'm only twenty-one. How old are you?'

'Fifty-three.' His legs became heavy and he sat back onto the warm bonnet. Loretta loomed over him and traced the lines around his eyes with her red painted fingernails. He flinched.

'So old. Too old for me. Pity. I liked you. Oh well, only one thing for it,' she said and stood tall. Dan stared without blinking when Loretta raised her hands to the sky and pirouetted on tiptoes. 'I'm the fairy on top of the tree. Do you see my wings? See how they shimmer in the moonlight.' At her words, the clouds dispersed and a bright full moon appeared. It shone down on Loretta as she danced, bathing her in an ethereal glow.

Dan thought she looked more like an angel than a fairy and despite his fear, smiled and clapped in rhythm to her twists and turns. She stopped and beckoned him to join her. His weighty limbs became light and he jumped away from the hood of the car as though he were eighteen again. Loretta held open her arms and he ran into her embrace. She tugged him close and he laid his head on her breast.

'Dance again.'

'Aw, no Honey. I'm all tired out.'

'Please. I need...I just want...'

'Oh, I know what you want.'

Dan lifted his head and stared into Loretta's black eyes. He saw something reflected in them and watched as a miniature movie played. He saw the Cadillac all new and waxed, pull up beside a snow covered line of trees. The wood was deserted and the exhaust sent up plumes of white smoke that disappeared into the crisp night air. He heard music play and like in a film, the focus of the scene changed from exterior to interior.

In the backseat of the car, a man, and a woman lay. The man's shirt was pulled out of his pants and he was fumbling around the woman's blouse trying to unbutton it.

'Come on, Baby, hurry up, I gotta get back before Hal gets home with the kids.'

'Goin' as fast as I can, Darlin'. Hey, give me a hand will ya?'

The woman swiped his fingers away and began to undo the buttons, but before she could get too far, the door flew open and Loretta dragged her out by her hair.

Loretta blinked and the image faded.

'When was the last time you and your wife did it?'

'What?'

'You know? Got all fleshy with each other?'

'I…well…we've been married for thirty years and you know, things change in a relationship. The sex side of things just well, fizzle out.'

Loretta pushed him. He tottered for a moment then regained his balance. She shook her head. 'Can't do it anymore eh? Sad. You're no use to me all out of practice.'

'Hey, I can still give a girl a good time.'

She laughed. He grabbed her by the arm and leaned towards her lips. She stopped him from kissing her with a click of her fingers. He stood upright as if struck by lightening.

'Amateur, pawing me like a lovesick schoolboy.' She turned and he followed, dragging his feet.

'I'm not a virgin you know.'

'What's that Hun?'

'I've been around. I've just had an affair.'

'Don't bother me with your indiscretions. Like I said, you're old. I thought you'd be a gentleman, but you're like all the rest.' Loretta walked away from him, shining the torch in front of her.

'No I'm not. Hey, where are you going? Don't leave me here.'

'Stop whining. Jeez, you're such a baby.'

'I'm not, I'm…'

'Quiet. I'm thinking,' she said, and turned around. She put her hands against her temples and began to fade into the darkness.

Dan blinked and rubbed his eyes. He stared at the strange woman as if he was looking through a sheet of gauze. 'Loretta?'

'Shhh, I'm thinking.'

He shivered and felt his gut turn over.

'This is ridiculous. What am I doing? Look, Loretta, maybe we should start walking. I passed some houses a couple of miles back. We can phone for a taxi.'

Loretta lowered her head. When she raised it again, her face was gaunt, her eyes intense and bloodshot. They bored into his sheepish gaze causing him to gasp. He noticed that she looked thinner than before, and less distinct as though she were disappearing.

The air became still.

Dan gulped. He tried to move, but his feet wouldn't budge. Loretta approached his rigid body, leaned in close to his ear and whispered, 'I don't do walking. Look at these shoes. Do you know how much they cost? Two weeks wages. Do you think that I would ruin them by trudging down a filthy road?' Dan swallowed. 'Get into the car,' she said and pushed him towards the door. He stumbled and fell to his knees. Loretta bent down and pulled him up by his hood.

'Get in.'

Dan heard the engine rev and looked down at Loretta's fingers. The knuckles were protruding from her greenish skin. He yanked his coat from her tight grip.

'What's happening to you?'

'Me? Not a thing, stud. Why don't you get into the car, now that it's all fixed.'

'It is?'

'Sure. Come on, I'll show you.'

Dan didn't move.

'What are you waiting for?'

'The breakdown truck.'

Loretta cocked her ear to one side and the low rumble sound of a heavy vehicle crept towards them. 'Oh, it must be them.'

'Thank God,' Dan said and peered into the distance. Two white lights appeared and he waved his arms. 'Here, over here!'

The roar of the truck was deafening. Hands over his ears, he jumped to the side of the road as it hurtled towards him as though he wasn't there. Dan fell against a wall of thick bramble and shouted, 'Come back! Hey!' The red taillights disappeared and Dan plodded back to where Loretta stood by the driver's door of the Cadillac. 'Why didn't they stop?'

'Maybe they didn't see you.'

'But I was in the middle of the road.'

'I know Honey, but it's so dark and you're so insignificant.'

'I am?'

'Oh, don't look so sad. Everything is fine. Come on, Honey, cheer up. After all, it's nearly Christmas.'

Dan smiled. 'Yes, it is, and I've got to get home and give Karen her present.'

Loretta squinted. 'Oh, her. Yep, she's got to have her gift. Come on, get in,' she said and opened the door. Dan clambered inside and she sat next to him. 'Move over Darln'. I'll drive.'

He shuffled sideways and Loretta held out her hand. 'Key'

'It's in the ignition, but it's no good it won't start, it's broken.'

'No, it isn't, it was working a few minutes ago wasn't it?'

'Well, yes, it was. But then it stopped.'

'I'll get it to work. I know what it takes to get her started.' Loretta turned the key. The engine shuddered into life and she pressed her foot on the accelerator.

'How did you do that? It's amazing. Okay,

thanks for getting it going, I'll take over now.'

Loretta gripped the steering wheel and shook her head. 'I don't think so. You see, this time, I'll do the driving.'

'What do you mean, "This time"?'

'He wouldn't let me drive. So I had to go everywhere by bus or taxi. That night, I caught a cab and walked the rest of the way. You know, he actually said, "Girls can't drive." But I did. In this very car.'

Dan's heart thumped as Loretta took the handbrake off. He grabbed the door handle and pushed. It was locked. He felt his head being thrown back as the Cadillac picked up speed. Loretta floored the accelerator pedal and Dan groped around for his seat belt.

'For God's sake, slow down, you'll kill us both!'

'No, Honey, not both.'

He saw the naked limbs of trees and twisted spiky bramble bushes flash past the window he desperately tried to open. Then he heard a splitting sound and turned his head. Appalled, he watched the bones of Loretta's finger burst through her skin.

'Just look at your face. Not going to be sick

are you?'

Dan was, all over the leather seats. He wiped his mouth and coughed. His eyes widened when he saw Loretta's face slowly shrivel and turn black. He pressed himself against the door and said, 'Oh god! What are you?'

'I'm Loretta. Been nice knowing you, Lover. Have a very Merry Christmas.'

Loretta took her bony hands off the steering wheel and leaned back. The car veered violently to the left. Skeletal fingers dug into his wrist. He tried to pull away, but her grip was strong. 'Sorry, sweetie, nothing you can do now. Why don't you sit right back and enjoy the ride?'

Dan screamed as the green sedan crashed into the side of a scarred tree trunk. His face smashed into the dashboard and blood poured from a deep cut on his forehead. Unable to move, he took short, painful breaths.

Through a red haze, he saw Loretta, restored to her former youthful guise, hurtle through the windscreen and land on top of the bonnet. Steam rose from either side of the hood and the engine cut. Loretta lay face down and melted into the silver statue.

'Woman in flight,' Dan said, just before his heart stopped beating.

SLEEPWALKING
Gillian Rennie-Dunkerley

For the first time in four years Florence Nightingale did not spend Christmas with us. Not the genuine article, of course, but a small, disturbed image of her manifested in my sister, Agnes. That final December appearance was explosive and left us all scarred in some way but I jump ahead and need to take you back to when Agnes first started grammar school and Miss Nightingale began her visits. It was a surprise to our parents that Agnes had passed the 11-plus exam as she was not interested in reading, her Maths was very weak and her general knowledge scant. While my brother and I would be happy to spend our spare time buried in books, Agnes would always be doing something practical. Making bizarre dolls out of rags, necklaces from flowers and painting our patient Labrador with water colours so that his golden coat became worthy of Joseph. She also loved cleaning and polished everything she could get hold of. My mother was probably grateful for this but we were all horrified when

Agnes decided one day to bath the budgie after cleaning out his cage. The poor creature did not survive his dunking in soapy water and the rigorous rub-down with a hankie.

Agnes was always happiest during the Summer holidays when she was free to pursue these diverse activities. Then she was charming, laughing and even entertaining. This changed as the date drew nearer for her to return to school Everyone in the family except me used to dread September and the gradual decline into Winter as the habits of Agnes became more and more disturbing particularly her nocturnal ones. I was merely fascinated and not in the least disturbed by the nightly excursions.

They would start quite quietly as the leaves on the horse-chestnut outside my window began to change colour and crisp at the edges. Being the youngest, I would be the first to go to bed then Agnes a couple of hours later. All would be peaceful until about half an hour after she had fallen asleep then the fun would begin. The nights would still be relatively warm so it might be that she took on the role of a wood nymph and skipped and cavorted along the landing swinging her nightdress in rhythm to a particularly tuneless song that she shrilled out of tune to accompany her dance. Or it might be that she was an animal - more often bearing a striking resemblance to our dog lumbering along. For this, she would be on all fours and heave her body from side to side to emulate the poor dog's ancient hips. Then she would slump to the floor, scratch behind her ear and curl up outside my parents' bedroom. All of these Autumnal twilight journeys were benign and harmless. My parents would be able to speak softly to her and persuade their sleeping daughter to return to bed and there would be no more visits that night.

However, as Autumn progressed and school became more demanding so her activities darkened and became more frantic. A favourite was to gather food from the pantry - usually a loaf of bread or a bunch of bananas - then creep into my parents' bedroom and stand at the end of the bed while they slept. She would tear off lumps of bread or take the banana skins and hurl them at my parents. She would always eat the bananas so some small comfort for the recipients of the ammunition. My father fixed locks on both the kitchen and pantry doors but then Agnes in her sleeping state would climb through the hatch from the dining room and force the pantry door open.

It seemed that as the Winter wore on Agnes gained more super powers in response to the pressures from school. Simultaneously, she was getting bad reports from school and my parents were invited in for an interview about her on several occasions. Her physical strength at night far exceeded her slight even puny adolescent daytime body. Despite bigger and more sophisticated locks, nighttime Agnes was determined to open all doors so my parents gave up and let her run free.

Agnes' experience at grammar school disintegrated. Her first year there was simply one of confusion; the second of anxiety with the third and fourth brewing up into a storm of resentment and finally anarchy against a system lacking sympathy for her. It was a constant battle between the school trying to confine Agnes within an academic structure and her trying to break every rule she could through her frustration and isolation. The other girls were quick and clever achieving gold stars and praise while Agnes simply received sarcastic comments and punishment for not understanding.

By November each year her obsession with Florence Nightingale would begin. When the house was quiet and everyone asleep, Agnes would raid the airing cupboard. Towels, bedding and other linen were tossed onto the landing then picked over until the most appropriate pieces were found. A white sheet wrapped around her body, a pink towel to be an apron and the crowning glory of a striped tea-towel knotted around her hair. How did we know she was Florence Nightingale? Because every night she would come into my room and sit on my bed telling me not to worry - Miss Nightingale was there to make me better. She would lift my arm to take my pulse, pull my six year old frame forward to examine my back and tap me with her fingertips before declaring that I was getting better. My parents, on hearing her rummaging in the cupboard would follow her, putting their fingers to their lips reminding me not to speak but let her end the performance herself. Then they would escort her back to her bed, divesting her of her robes along the way while she gave them their orders for the next patient. The following day she would have no recollection of any of this and my mother would simply tidy the airing cupboard for the next outing.

I was not scared of my sister's regular visits but just accepted it as the norm. My parents, however, were concerned and invited a psychiatrist to witness the events. At her usual time, Agnes appeared in full Florence Nightingale attire.

'Beware that man!' She shouted and pointed and kept repeating until he left.

December that year was the worst. It was a particularly harsh and early winter with snow and ice a feature before Christmas chilling us all in the days before central heating. The climax occurred on a deeply frosty night. My brother who was two years older than Agnes had been a constant target for her crepuscular outings. She would go into his bedroom and rearrange his possessions sometimes even removing them. They would turn up later in the most unlikely places some even in the dog's basket though it was a tight squeeze. He had little patience with her and there would be terrible arguments during the day that would end with Agnes sobbing and pleading innocence. My father decided a further lock was needed on my brother's door. That evening my brother had left to stay with a friend. In the early hours I woke up to hear violent crashing and screaming. I peeped out of my door to witness the scene. Agnes in her super-power state had ripped the door open of my brother's bedroom and had snatched anything she could - books, records, files of schoolwork - and tossed them over the banisters. My parents were trying to calm and distract her but she was like a demon intent on her mission. Papers were fluttering like confetti as she shrieked with delight. Finally, with a great roar, she flung the bedclothes to one and grabbed the mattress. To our amazement she dragged it out of the room, tipped it on one side and pushed it down the stairs. We all watched in silence and disbelief. She returned to the room and started pushing the bed frame when she suddenly stopped upon seeing me standing there clutching my father in fright. She was then immediately composed, walked to me and bustled me back to bed, tucking me in like one of her patients.

Something had to be done. I remember my mother sobbing and my father shaking his head at the destruction. Where did this immense strength come from? It is only all these years later that I can realise the fear and hopelessness my parents must have felt. Was their daughter mad? What had they done wrong to produce such violence? Upon his return, my brother was furious. All his studious notes had been torn and thrown away. His precious record collection smashed and his clothes flung out of the wardrobe. The crowning glory was seeing his bed scattered around the house. Another psychiatrist visited and he also investigated how Agnes behaved at school. My parents were besides themselves with worry but a decision was reached by all three parties. Agnes was to leave school immediately and not return. She was fifteen.

January saw a new Agnes. Christmas had been very peaceful. Florence did not appear and the dog was able to have her basket to herself without a record or book squashed in beside her. My brother grudgingly agreed to leave his door unlocked although he took the precaution of a booby trap inside the room just in case. It was not set off. My mother had found Agnes a job as an assistant in a care home and she thrived. Since the day she left school Agnes has not walked in her sleep again but has gone on to carve out a very successful career as a highly qualified and respected nurse specialising in mental health. Years of dedication and studying with sympathetic teachers achieved this. She is exemplary in her practice of listening to her patients and teasing out the deeply hidden reasons for their misery and trauma. As for Florence Nightingale – she's firmly in the airing cupboard and in the past.

SLEIGH JINGLE
Judith Osborne

Appalachian sky of medieval
Stained glass blue
Backdrops the ragged silhouettes of
Pine tree heads,
Forests attached on slopes, on rocks, on
Whitened heights
On even the gold, magnetic disc of
Slowly falling sun.
At ten below a mildish winter evening
At a meter deep a moderate snow,
The fall of Sunday last.
Now snow on snow and ice on ice
In shafts and glows of window lights
Sparkles, glitters, gleams and crunches,
Packed under tyres, under feet, under blades.
Distant faint orchestral timpani
Tickle the eardrums, excite the nerves,
Twitch the feet and fingers –
Sleighbells!
Christmas Tree Day, that was the promise –
Purchase not involved, but sleighbells!
Finger shadows lengthen;
At street corners, on the playground,
Circled by gusts of laughter,

Pummelled by fisted snowballs,
Snowmen stand guard.
Gates stand open, drive swept clear,
Lamplit on either side;
White pillars please the eye, the door
Holds close all those inside.
Dog faces at the window stare,
Decide to raise alarms –
"Hurray, you're here! Come in,
Be welcome and be warm,
Logs are cracklin', supper's a cookin',
Mulled wine's on the hob;
Goodies a plenty, no stintin' for our guests!"
Hospitable warm embraces,
Glad cries from hot hearthside
Three generations of Virginians engulf
Two Brits in seasonal charm.
'Now here's the toast, and here's the toast –
To Britons now, and then! Raise a glass
And down a glass, we'll forge another link
To bind old Jamestown settlers with you
Who show up now.
Come on then, folks – the highlight next –
Let's go get the Christmas tree!'
A torchlight line heads stablewards,
Horse neighs assail the ears.
Once through the yard and in the barn
Good horse smells fill the nose,
Straw rustles, hoof scrapes,
Warm flanks close by to pat,

'Leroy my beauty, your star turn,
It's up and off we go –
The sleigh, belled harness,
Our guests and us.
Let's not forget the saw!'
Knees tightly wrapped, noses red,
Mouths stretched in gleeful grins
Seven adults yell like fourteen kids
To feel the freezing breeze rush by
And hear the sleighbells jing.
'Our Christmas tree, our Christmas tree,
All hands to our stations!
Pile out, jump down, this won't take long –
You've seen the yellow bow.
Our trusty saw will make short work –
Ah timber! there she goes!
Great care, now wrap, tie, hoist!'
Aboard the trailer hooked astern.
Moon pierced, star spangled sky
And banner frothing,
Leroy trots back, the tree behind,
Soft darkness crowds around.
A chimney smokes, ten windows glow,
The house stands foursquare safe.
Fling wide the door and tumble in –
Sing sweet a Christmas carol,
Bring strings of twinkle-coloured lights and
Sparkle-silver baubles.
Breathe deep of pine and spicy wine,
Jazz round our noble tree.

Catch the beat, hit the note –
The chandeliers may fall!
Sound joy and peace, Virginia –
A blessing on us all!

Another Christmas Eve
Will Ingrams

Percival Hood's long nose tingled as he stepped out into the frosty night air. He pulled the door closed behind him and buttoned his coat over last year's Christmas scarf. He hoped for a new cardigan tomorrow. *Hmm, nineteen sixty seven nearly through,* he reflected, carefully avoiding the ice by the school gate, *where do the years go?* Percy glanced across the boys' playground through the blackened brick arch, beyond the streetlight's misty white realm. His dispersing breath-cloud revealed the outline of the climbing frame.

'Evening Sir.'

'Dempsey? What on earth are you doing up there? Why aren't you at home, waiting for Father Christmas to call?'

'That's a load of crap. Sorry Sir, rubbish.'

'But you must be freezing Dempsey! Not even a coat on. Get home to your father, boy.'

'Can't Sir. Did that last year, an 'e wasn't there. Staggered 'ome after midnight and started 'itting me, Sir. Knocked me down, Mister 'Ood.'

'Good God, Dennis! That's appalling. Come down, boy, and I'll walk home with you now. I'd like to speak with your father.'

'Won't do no good Sir.' Dennis climbed slowly down. Percy took the boy's thin arm and walked him through the black iron gate. He looked down at Dennis Dempsey, the streetlight revealing a round pale face marked by dark bruises. The teacher tutted, fresh anger rising, but his attention was snatched away by a garbled shout.

'Oi! Dennis! That you? Get 'ere ya little weasel!'

A drunken Dempsey shambled towards them, hurling threats. Hood pushed the boy behind him, expecting harsh words but clenching a fist just in case. He stood firm and looked at the drunkard down his long nose, but he never stood a chance. Dempsey raised his right as he rushed forward and swung at Hood's face; no words.

Percy knew he should be falling painfully but felt absolutely nothing. The fist, the arm and the man passed right through him with hardly a flutter and Dempsey just vanished.

'Good Lord! What on earth just happened?'

'Sorry 'bout that Mister 'Ood. Me Dad fell down after 'e beat me last year. Smashed his 'ead on the door step, stone dead. But 'e keeps coming back like that. Terrifies me Sir, can't sleep some nights. Sorry.'

'What? That was a ghost, Dennis? Good God. I was absolutely convinced! I've never...

But Dennis, I didn't know of your loss, I'm so sorry. Whatever happened to you after that?'

'Me Grandma moved in. Lived round the corner before, Sir.'

'Well I never. My condolences, Dennis. What a terrible thing to happen, and I didn't even know. But here, up on that climbing frame tonight? Why?'

'Just looking at the moon, Sir. Calm and peaceful. They really going to send men up there soon, the Americans? I'd love to be one of them astronauts.'

Percy looked down at the boy's moonlit face, the dark eyes wide. He nodded and smiled encouragingly.

'You're a bright boy Dempsey, sharp at arithmetic. With application and continued study, there's no reason why you shouldn't make something of yourself. Perhaps you could train to become an astronaut one day.'

'No sir, I can't possibly. Not now.'

'Why not, boy? What do you mean?'

'Cos it was my fault Mister 'Ood. Once 'e knocked me down, I 'it 'im with the poker, buckled his knee. I made 'im die, Sir. They don't send you up there if you kill people, do they? Only way's down for me, now.'

'No, no Dennis, you mustn't think like that. It was just a terrible accident. You shouldn't assume all the blame. Look, I'm going to take you back to your grandmother. I want to speak with her.'

'No Sir. It won't do no good.'

'Dennis, I insist. I need to see her.' Hood took the boy's arm again but he resisted, looking up with worried, pleading eyes.

'Please Sir, don't. Thing is, you're not the first to know the truth, Mister 'Ood. I told me Grandma tonight too – 'ow 'er son knocked me down last Christmas Eve. 'Ow I reached for the poker and swung at 'is legs, so 'e fell.'

'Well Dennis, it's always best for boys to tell the truth. Have things clear, set out in black and white.'

'No Sir, it wasn't. She got really angry when I told 'er. Started shaking me. 'Urt me, she did.'

'And is that why you ran to school, to get away from her?'

'Yes Sir. After she fell.'

'Your grandmother fell down? Was she hurt?'

Before Dennis could respond they were hailed from further along the street. Hood looked up to see a slight figure, an elderly lady bundled up in a black coat and scarf. She hobbled towards them leaning on a stick.

'Is that your grandmother, Dennis? Come on, I can speak with her now.'

The boy turned away from Percy's searching gaze. Hood took his arm again and walked towards the advancing figure, dragging his reluctant pupil along. Her croaked words were clearer now, 'Dennis? You're a wicked boy!'

It took Percy a second to register that there was no pale breath-cloud as she spoke, and he paused, struck with new fear. Hood seized the boy with both hands, bent towards him, 'You didn't strike your grandmother too, did you boy? Tell me this isn't another ghost!'

Even as Percy's grip tightened on his thin arms, Dennis twisted and struggled free, diving between the teacher's legs to escape, destabilising him. Before Percy could recover, the grandmother figure was upon him and he shrank away, glancing back towards the pale cone of light by the school gate. Dennis had vanished from sight. The grandmother raised her stick but Percy also sensed a movement low down to his side. He turned to see Dennis lunging forward swinging a broken iron railing, dark in his white fists.

The crack of Percy's head striking the dull grey flagstones rang clear down the moonlit street; a frosty, deserted street.

SPEED
Mike Moody

Ian sat in his car looking out at the building in front of him, the one in which he was about to learn about speed awareness. He'd only been driving for thirty five years so of course he knew nothing about speed! The rain ran down the windscreen, making the scene in front blurry. A bit like his mind at that moment.

What was the point? Well the point was it would save him collecting three points on his licence. No matter what he was taught a slight lapse of attention and he could end up going thirty five in a thirty limit again.

Be positive, said one side of him. But what a waste of time said the other.

Well it may be of some interest to people in the local since a few of them have been on similar sessions. I seem to remember their view of the course was negative. Hope I can take back something more positive, but I doubt it.

Ian looked at his watch. It was time to go and register for the training session. He dashed through the rain reaching the entrance only to find it shut. He was dripping wet but then saw there was a button to press which alerted the reception area. He pushed it and peered through the glass door towards what looked like the reception. A face appeared at the sliding glass window and smiled at him.

Just open the door will you, silly cow.

There was a click and the door opened. He entered, dripping all over the floor.

'Please don't move off the mat. If you drip over the tiled floor I'll have to mop it up. It's a safety hazard you know. People might slip and injure themselves.'

Ian stared at her while he dripped slowly on the mat.

Is she nuts? What's she going to do if several people come in? Have them queuing outside. This is not a good start.

'Perhaps I can take your details while you are stood there?'

A number of people sitting in the waiting area were staring at him with big grins on their faces.

'Are you on the speed awareness course?'

'Yes'

'Your name, please.'

Ian glared at the receptionist but she was oblivious.

'Ian Jones'

'Oh yes. You're on the list. Now, if you wouldn't mind, please shake your coat on the mat and then you may put it in the cloakroom which is next to the toilets, the first turning to the left.'

She turned her back to him and walked off to return to her cosy office, clearly not made at all uncomfortable by the look of daggers focused on her.

'Just like being back at school, eh?'

Ian turned and saw a large, grey-haired bloke smiling at him from the waiting area.

'Yeah. I feel I'm about ten years old. Must get this wet coat off - without wetting the floor.'

He shook his coat over the mat and made his way to the cloakroom leaving his coat there to dry.

'You can get a hot drink from the vending machine. It's free.'

'Thanks, mate. I could do with a hot drink after that soaking.'

He got himself a hot coffee and sat by the

grey-haired chap.

'Are you here for the speed awareness course? '

'Yeah. I think we all are from what I've heard.'

As their conversation continued they discovered where and at what speed they had been caught. It turned out they had both been caught by a mobile speed trap whilst travelling at thirty five in a thirty limit, following other traffic.

'Seems like there's been a bit of a crackdown, with the number of people here.'

'Yeah. A lot of hassle for everyone. I mean why not give us a warning and a fine if it happens again. Particularly in the circumstances we were caught in. All the bureaucracy and time involved in organising these courses. Of course people are going to attend to avoid getting points on their licence. But I doubt if the course is going to be of any use.'

'True. Hang on. Looks like we might have a female wrestler to run the course!'

A tall, well built woman had walked into the waiting area. She wore a tight suit with an open necked shirt. Her muscles bulged in the tight fabric.

'Good morning,' she boomed.

All heads turned and talking stopped.

'I'm taking the speed awareness course. Follow me please.'

Ian finished his drink quickly.

'We'd better move. I don't fancy getting on the wrong side of her.'

They all trudged into the classroom and found seats for themselves.

The female tutor introduced herself as Stella Rudd. She advised that she was an advanced driver and that, as well as taking speed awareness courses, she was a part time HGV driver. Very appropriate, Ian thought.

'I'd like to take your names to ensure everyone is here. Please answer when I say your name.'

The roll call was completed and it was found two people were missing. If they didn't turn up they forfeited their fee and could end up with points and a fine on top.

'We'll start by you all introducing yourselves and stating why you are here. If the missing people don't arrive within this period of time then they will not be allowed in the class.'

All twenty five people were there for reasons very similar to Ian. Most said it was due to a lack of attention because they were talking to a passenger or had been distracted by something. However, there was one lady aged about sixty with a rather posh accent, who flatly denied doing anything wrong.

'My name is Celia Hamilton-Smith and I have been accused of breaking the speed limit in my very own village of Chestleton. Of course this is complete nonsense. I would never do such a thing and I am only here because I had advice that it would be the best way to deal with the matter. Apparently a recording from a piece of electronic equipment, probably assembled in the third world, is better than my word.'

Ian was about to say something, but thought it better to keep his views to himself.

Do we have to sit and listen to this drivel. Silly woman. Unbelievable!

There were a few chuckles in the class and the tutor stood there open mouthed. After a quiet minute she started to speak.

'Well Celia I..'

'Excuse me Ms Rudd will you be kind enough to refer to my title and surname, Mrs Hamilton-Smith, if you don't mind.'

Ian turned and looked at the woman.

Title! Talk about hyphenated snobs!

Other people in the class were now looking open-eyed, some at Mrs Hamilton-Smith and some at Ms Rudd.

Stella's face flushed and Ian, sitting at the front, could see her left lower eyelid twitch. She was keeping her temper under control, but for how long Ian wondered.

'Mrs Hamilton-Smith I believe you are here because you have been caught breaking the speed limit. If you cannot accept that then I suggest you leave the class and take the matter up with the Police Authority.'

'Well of course I accept it. Can you not see that I am here? Does that not mean that I accepted my invitation to come on this course? You asked people to state why they were here and I am only giving you the facts as I understand them. I do not believe that I was travelling more than thirty and....'

Stella's face had gradually reddened and she

started to cut Mrs Hamilton-Smith short, 'Mrs Ham....'

'Hello. Bit late. Sorry to interrupt.' The door had opened and a young man burst in. He didn't look eighteen, having a baby face and a plumpish stature. His t shirt was a bit short and his bare belly hung over his belt. When he saw the height and muscular physique of the tutor he stood still, having decided not to say anymore. Standing with his mouth open he awaited some words from the tutor.

Mrs Hamilton-Smith saw her opportunity, 'As I was saying, I am sure I was driving within the speed limit. I have never in my life driven above the speed limit.'

Ian smiled for the first time since he arrived.

I didn't expect entertainment to be part of the course.

Stella stood looking from Mrs H to the young man who had just arrived. She decided to turn to Mrs H.

'Mrs Hamilton-Smith I will address your comment once I have admitted this young man to the class.'

She turned around with her back to Mrs H.

'Your name, please.'

'Stephen, but most people call me Steve. Sorry I'm late missus. Got stuck in traffic and didn't dare put me foot down to make it up. You know with the class and all.'

'Your full name please, Stephen.'

'Oh! Yeah, course, it's Stephen Wellington. Good name on a day like this, eh? You know, rain and all.'

Stephen didn't get a laugh or any sign of a smile from Stella.

'Please sit down. You have made it just in time. Now let the class know why you are here.'

Stephen looked at Stella with mouth open. The rest of the class stared at him.

'Well?'

'Sorry missus, I thought we were all here for speeding. Didn't they tell you?'

'I am fully aware of that but I'm asking you to tell us why in particular you are here. Where and why were you speeding?'

'Well, I was on the A12 and just going with the flow. Didn't know I was speeding. Didn't think I was. If I was then all the rest of them were and...'

'Do we have to listen to this drivel? This

individual is unable to understand or communicate effectively I am sure we all have more important things to do.'

Heads turned in astonishment at yet another interruption from this unlikeable lady. Ian was about to say something to her but with Mrs Hamilton-Smith staring directly at him he decided it would just prolong things.

Doesn't she know when to keep her mouth shut? About time she got the boot.

Stella walked two paces forward and stood in front of Mrs Hamilton-Smith.

'Mrs Hamilton-Smith I am running this class. If you do not wish to attend then leave now and I will mark you as not attending and you will receive points and a fine.'

'I certainly don't want to leave. I've had to re-arrange some important appointments to come on this course.'

Ian was thinking that the class might turn out more entertaining than he had expected.

Stella stared at her for a while and then spoke loud and slow. 'Then you had better keep quiet until I speak to you.'

Ian had turned round to see how Mrs H would react. She started to open her mouth when she saw Ian put a finger to his mouth. No sound came out. She seemed to have come to her senses and decided to keep quiet.

'OK, class. The first thing I would like you to learn about is the effects of speeding….'

'We all know that don't we missus. You might get caught and get points on your licence. Then if you get caught again…'

'Stephen! You will only speak when you are asked to. I will teach, you will listen and then you will speak when I ask you to. Do you understand?'

'Should you be talking to him like that? None of us are children and we should be treated with respect.'

'Mrs Hamilton – Smith, out of my class now. I will not be told by you or anyone how I should deal with attendees of this class who, by the way, volunteered to come.'

'But I..'

Stella went up to Mrs Hamilton –Smith and looked her in the face and said firmly, 'Out now!'

In shock, Mrs Hamilton – Smith got out of her seat and made a quick exit. But before shutting the door she shouted, 'I will write to my MP about this.'

Stella glared at her as the door shut.

Ian whispered to his neighbour, 'I hope we can get on with this nonsense now that up-her-own-arse snob has gone.'

Stella turned back to the class.

'Now does anyone else want to argue with me?'

The class remained silent and Stella began her lesson advising on the effects of hitting objects at various speeds and braking distances. She asked if anyone had been involved in an accident. Ian had and was asked to tell his tale.

'The road was quite busy and me and the wife were in a small Fiat provided by a garage while my vehicle was in for a service. We were driving towards a roundabout at the end of a dual carriageway. I slowed down and came to a stop to be sure no traffic was coming. Then there was a thud and the next thing I was half way on the roundabout completely stunned. As I came around I saw cars at a standstill and some people getting out of their cars. Somebody asked if we were ok. Having just come to our senses we were still taking in what had happened. To cut the story short the driver behind said he had been looking at traffic on the roundabout and thought that I wouldn't need to stop. So he hit me at something like 20 or 30 mph. Not only did it cause a lot of hassle with a damaged car and insurance claims to sort out, my wife had been bruised and I had a bad neck for a month after. If we hadn't had seat belts on it would have been much worse.'

'Thanks for your contribution, Ian. This just shows that hitting something at a relatively slow speed can have serious consequences. The higher the speed the more serious the consequences.'

Just as Stella was about to start her next subject the receptionist entered the classroom.

'Stella, I have a lady in the reception area demanding that she speaks to someone senior. I have tried to explain that we are a facility which rents rooms out, but she just won't go.'

'Well she cannot return to this class. She is too disruptive and she has been dismissed. If she has complaints she must take it to the Police Authority.'

'Thank you. I'll make it clear to her.'

As she was about to walk out Mrs

Hamilton-Smith returned to the classroom. Just as she was about to speak Stella turned towards her, saying authoratively , 'Out Mrs Hamilton-Smith! Talk to your MP if you wish, but do not bother me anymore with your interruptions.'

'May I get my handbag? I left it by my seat.'

In exasperation, Stella manged to say, 'Yes. Get it and go.'

Mrs Hamilton-Smith walked to her chair, bent down and picked up her handbag. All eyes were on her with an expectation that she would say something. But she stared at Stella, huffed and walked to the door.

'Been nice to meet you, Mrs H. You've brightened my day.'

Everyone turned and stared at Stephen.

'What?'

'Stephen, I do not want any more interruptions. All they are doing is delaying the finish time of this class. I have a number of topics to cover and you will not exit this classroom until I have finished. Now can we get on with things?'

After that the course went smoothly. The effects of accidents were shown, the importance of stopping distances and the recognition of dangers. Various questions and answer sessions made the subjects more interesting. Ian found it surprising to see what poor knowledge a lot of the people had and he also learnt that his own knowledge was not one hundred percent despite the high mileage he travelled.

By the end Ian felt it had been quite enlightening and not the nonsense he had expected. It had cost him an afternoon but he had prevented points being put on his licence and in truth the course had been both interesting and entertaining, particularly so with the antics of Mrs Hamilton-Smith.

As luck would have it he hit the roads at a busy time and progress home was slow. At one point the traffic queue was going at a snail's pace. Up ahead he could see a police car and an ambulance alongside another two cars and a police officer directing traffic around the accident spot. As he approached the two cars, one a big Mercedes and the other an Astra, he saw that there was a woman standing by the Merc arguing with a police officer. The large Mercedes had apparently run into the back of the smaller Astra. The damage was significant albeit they were in a 30 mph limit. As he was crawling past he saw that the woman talking to the police officer was Mrs Hamilton-Smith. She was handing a mobile phone to the officer, but talking all the while. With his window down he heard part of their conversation.

'Mrs Hamilton-Smith, will you accept that you were on your phone when this accident occurred?'

'I certainly will not officer. Of course I was holding it because it rang and it may have been important......' Ian heard no more and drove on thinking, *She never gives up and seems to have received the comeuppance she deserves.*

Driving home he felt content. He had only gone on the course to avoid having points on his licence but he had learnt something from the course, there had been entertainment and an unlikeable woman had got what she deserved. All in all it should make a good tale to share with his mates in the pub that evening.

WINTER'S CRUELTY
Gillian Rennie-Dunkerley

'Nice day for it,' chuckled Ian to himself as if he didn't say the same thing every single morning. Jane smiled thinly and slapped the butter extra hard onto her toast.

'Going for your usual constitution this morning, dear?'

'Oh, I expect so.'

Jane <u>knew</u> so. How she longed to escape from this dreary brown house and her dreary brown husband and spend time with Daniel. They may only be able to snatch ten minutes or so but what wonderful minutes they were.

'Same old walk, is it? I'd get bored myself – don't know why you bother.'

Jane could have replied that it was so that she could meet up with the most extraordinary man who made her come alive but instead she just smiled.

'Cheerio.' The door slammed behind her.

***

The sky was free of clouds. Baby-blue with soft puffs of pink on the horizon. The sun was not up but the golden light slowly, seductively melting across the landscape promised it soon would be. It was cold. Fingers of ice hung down from the sides of the hedge - strings of bramble like pearl necklaces swung languorously among the branches. Underfoot tiny ridges of mud peaked into frozen tips, crunching as Jane made her way across the footpath. Each breath in was sharp, cold, an intrusion in the heat of her lungs. Each breath out, a vapour trail. Jane walked quickly - her fingertips tingling and her exposed face pricking with the cold. Her brightly coloured padded jacket restricted her arms - swoosh, swoosh as she moved them against her unnaturally rounded, puffed body. It was a glorious morning. Her spirits soared as she lifted her face to the newly risen sun that was still low in the sky but splendid in its presence. There had been a week of fog and gloom but now all was forgotten in this twinkling, translucent day.

Jane reached the end of the field stepping onto the hard tarmac of the lane and couldn't resist slowly easing her heavily-booted foot - first the heel then smashing down the toe onto a large frozen puddle. It creaked and groaned at the resistance then splintered with shards splashing outwards. In contrast, the water underneath the icy layer was dark and muddy; the broken ice was virgin, pure with tinges of blue. Jane smiled to herself - why can't we resist breaking icy puddles? She continued on her way absorbed in the rejoicing birdsong that filled the air from the trees lining the lane. Looking up, the branches formed scars against the sky while tiny crystals delicately dripped as the warmth of the sun gently melted the frost.

A figure appeared around the corner. Small, bundled, difficult to determine its gender. It was walking very fast. Suddenly, a squeal (female, then), a flailing of limbs and a thud. As if in response, a startled pheasant thrashed through the undergrowth nearby, its ugly, urgent squawk signalling its affront. Jane hurried to help the fallen woman but was also cautious of the ice underfoot. The woman was lying on her side. Her right leg was angled outwards awkwardly. Jane put her thickly gloved hand to her mouth. The woman was moaning and crying - her shouts ringing through the clear air. Jane quickly pulled herself together and assessed the situation.

'It's okay. I'll 'phone 999 immediately.' She peeled off her glove and pulled her mobile from its resting place in her jacket. Her fingers were rapidly cooling down while she tapped the keys but she was connected quickly. A few details about how the woman had fallen heavily on the ice with directions to a remote lane near Bradbourne and Jane clicked the 'phone off, promptly pushing her chilled hand back into the glove. She bent down to help the woman.

'It's okay. Someone's coming. They may be a little while but they are coming.' She hoped she sounded calm and convincing while, in fact, she was actually very anxious and unsure of what to do. The woman stared up at her. Her skin was very white and stretched tightly over her skull. Her frightened eyes were dark and pleading. Tears were streaming down her face dripping onto her collar making the fur flat and wet. Her mouth opened as if to speak but only a piteous groan came out. She tried to move but that only released a piercing yell of pain.

'Just stay still - don't try to move.' Jane took the woman's hand in an effort to soothe her but as both were wearing such thick gloves a clasp was impossible.   She was anxious that the woman did not go into shock or become too cold. Jane knew she had to keep her warm and try to distract her but the temperature in this shady part of the lane was close to freezing. Jane did not recognise the woman - in fact, she was sure she had not seen her around the village before.

'Do you live nearby? Is there someone I can contact?'

The woman's eyes closed for a moment as shooting pain raked over her face.   Her lips were tightly pressed together and turning blue.

'In my pocket,' she murmured. Tentatively, trying not to make the woman move at all, Jane began the search. The first pocket - the one most exposed - was empty so Jane gently felt the other side of the thick, woollen coat. Eventually finding one, Jane squeezed her hand into the small flap and closed her fingers over a scrap of paper. She had been expecting at least a 'phone but teased the paper out carefully so as not to tear it.   Her gloved fingers clumsily unfolded the paper to reveal a name and address on it written in thick, bold letters:

DANIEL PERRY. OAK FARM

Jane stared at the words. Daniel Perry? The familiar name shook her. At first, she could not take them in then was confused, bewildered. She glanced at the woman. Who was she?

'Daniel Perry?' She queried. 'Do you know him?'

The woman gave a deep sigh. 'He's my husband,' she whispered. She squirmed with the pain and turned her head away. Jane looked at the woman lying there - and was both horrified and filled with guilt. A ripple of fear reverberated through her and she felt a trickle of panic beginning to creep along and stiffen her limbs. She scrunched the paper into a tight ball and stared down at the grass on the verge, frozen into white bristles to form a solid brush mat. A frost-covered stick, half-hidden, black underneath but with a white cover of frozen moss, poked out of the grass. Its forked branches seemed to be pointing accusingly at her.

Bang!

A bird-scarer exploded nearby and a cacophony of raucous cawing filled the air as a black cloud of rooks slowly flapped overhead. There were scuttles of unseen creatures in the hedge scurrying to safety. Jane became aware of the icy cold penetrating her body. The day was no longer a joy but a threat with the sun losing its temporary brilliance - its rays feeble and ineffective.

Jane looked at the woman again. Her eyes were closed and she appeared to be slipping asleep or unconscious. Jane acted instinctively.

'Wake up!' She lightly shook the woman. 'Oh, do wake up.'

The woman's eyelashes fluttered then her eyes slowly opened.

'Oh, thank goodness,' breathed Jane. 'Do try to stay awake. I'll just put my coat around you to help keep you warm,' she said while slipping off her padded jacket and folding it over the woman's body. Immediately, Jane began to shiver as she took the woman's hand in hers - 'They'll soon be here,' she said more to comfort herself than the woman. Time seemed to stand still and the temperature felt to be dropping rapidly but it was only a few minutes before

Jane heard a vehicle approach, whooshing through the icy puddles then the flash of yellow, white and blue ambulance. Two paramedics slammed out of the car and raced over to the woman who was now shaking uncontrollably. After a few words with them, Jane stepped back from the scene having rescued her coat and gratefully easing herself back into it. Heavy grey clouds had crept across the sky from the east and the sun was being suffocated by their pillowing effect. She turned away. Her mouth was dry, her thoughts racing as to the consequences of this discovery of Daniel's wife while opening the contacts list on her 'phone. Finding the name she pressed to dial. An immediate answer.

'Daniel...yes, yes, of course. I know you do...no, listen, something's happened. No, I'm fine,' Jane paused. 'It's not me... it's your wife...'

****

Daniel slowly returned the mobile to his pocket and gazed out of the window across the yard. What was she doing? Pulling out a heavy oak chair from behind the table he slumped into it and held his head in his hands as if the burden of thought was too much. He sat there for a long time while threads of solutions tangled themselves into knots in his mind. Was Rosa really here? Their arrangement was purely business. She wanted British Citizenship and he needed the money and they had got away with the deception for three years now. The last time he saw Rosa was their wedding day when they ridiculed the marriage vows then went their separate ways immediately afterwards – Rosa to Yorkshire and him left with a fat bundle of notes that certainly eased the financial pain of the farm. He hadn't given Rosa a second thought and then he met Jane and she made his life complete. Or she would if she divorced that boring idiot of a husband. But would Jane believe him and even if she did what would she think of him now? He realised that the whole episode was a terrible mistake as most of his actions in life seemed to be. He looked around the kitchen at the piles of dishes precariously balanced by the sink needing attention; the unopened post; the puddle of clothes on the floor next to the washing machine. Everything was a mess but Jane was the one light. He truly loved her. So why had he kept this from her? He buried his head in his hands again.

Jane no longer noticed her surroundings. The walk home was merely a practised routine – one foot in front of the other. The clouds had completely obliterated the sun now and the heavy pall of the winter's day smothered her. Her mind, however, was electric bright with sparks of reasons and explanations darting across each other. She had been such a fool, a love-sick, middle-aged woman who should know better. Of course he was married and he was just playing with her. He would have been bored with her soon anyway. Look at her – shapeless and saggy, a lined face and whispers of grey in her hair. You stupid, stupid woman. Tears of humiliation and self-pity gushed hotly down her face. Reaching the gate to her home she paused and stared at the familiar red-bricked house in front of her. When she left it this morning it had been like skipping to freedom now it beckoned her back to its comforting and dependable haven. She quietly opened the kitchen door hoping she could escape to the bathroom to wash her face. She closed her eyes as a sob shuddered through her body.

'You've been gone a long time,' Ian's voice drifted out from the sitting room.

Only yesterday, everything about him irritated and annoyed her as she compared him to the intense, passionate Daniel. The last eighteen months had been pure joy. Delicious and exciting – the chase from Daniel and then the intensity of their love. Or so she had thought but how could he have deceived her for so long and why? He knew she was married so why did he keep his marriage a secret? The answer hammered home – because he wanted to – because she, Jane, was merely a temporary distraction and he was really devoted to his wife. The pain of this knowledge shot through her. She was punctured by the revelation that she had been used and that now all she had left was this.

'Fancy a cup of tea, dear? Pop the kettle on, will you. "Homes Under the Hammer" has just started. Everything alright? Good walk?'

Jane sat on a kitchen chair.

'Yes, it was fine. I'm fine.'

Song of Christmas Angels
Joan Roberts

Seraphina sat strumming her golden harp praying for guidance to overcome the problems that lay ahead for this year's singing competition. Hope, one of the choir's most beautiful and important voices, had caught a chill and could barely speak. There had been frequent, violent storms causing the darker clouds of Violence, Hatred, Greed and Corruption to gather around and beneath them, pushing their much lighter cloud Nine higher towards the Sun and further from the Earth. This made it difficult for the choir's voices to be heard. A new cloud on the horizon, Globalisation, had raised Hope's spirits for a while and she had rallied briefly. Unfortunately, as the cloud approached and she saw the dark angels Hate and Avarice inhabit the lighter parts, creating thick dark patches, Hope's strength waned. The grey and gloomy prospect of yet another barrier had become almost too much to bear.

'Seraphina, I'm so sorry to interrupt. You

were playing such a sad melody. Have you had more bad news?' said the sweet voice of Charity.

'I was thinking about the Choir's great challenge this year. We need Hope so much.'

'Love, Faith and I were going to visit her today, why don't you come with us?'

Faith, Love and Charity had been away for most of the year, finding pockets of clear sky. They had been singing lullabies to those who had been affected by the dark cloud of Austerity, the grey spin-off from Globalisation. Seraphina considered Charity's brave blue eyes. Despite her enormous struggle, year in and out, she had maintained incredible fortitude. She had tirelessly campaigned to be heard above the deep bass tones of Hatred and Violence; her voice gaining in strength and beauty as she challenged the division and intolerance they had created.

The grey, menacing cloud Radicalisation was getting bigger as it came closer. Faith's good intentions had been deliberately misinterpreted by Hate, creating confusion and fear. Love and Charity were really struggling to be heard above its thunderous demons. They needed Hope more than ever. Seraphina would go with them to visit Hope, who might gain strength from Charity's unbelievable commitment.

Seraphina's spirits had been lifted by Charity's optimism and they practised a brief harmony during the short walk to the sunniest part of Cloud Nine.

'Don't get up Hope,' said Love as they approached her bright aura. 'We have brought you a present and I know it will help your voice.' Love produced a golden goblet into which she poured a honey coloured, creamy liquid, with a slight aura of its own.

'What is it?' croaked Hope.

'It's the milk of human kindness, of course,' laughed Faith. 'It's not so hard to find if you know where to look. We found it in the most unlikely places. It was the major cure for the Ebola epidemic.'

'There was quite a bit produced by some of the poorest people,' Charity explained. 'They showed remarkable kindness to thousands escaping the most despicable followers of Hate and Violence the world has seen in years. The people who have nothing to give share whatever they have. Those who have the most are often scared to give anything, in case they are being tricked. I know it will make you better, we have so much work to do.'

Hope drank sufficient and offered the goblet around the small group, each one taking a sip of the silky smooth, delicious nectar. Feeling delightfully refreshed, they took up their harps and started to sing. A glorious, harmonious sound filled the skies. Hope started to get to her feet. Her face shone in the radiance of the sun as she lifted her head high and sang with them. As her beautiful, soprano falsetto echoed beyond Cloud Nine, Seraphina knew that this year's competition would be their best yet.

FRAMGNAM MAN'S CHRISTMAS BONUS
Mike Moody

Jim didn't feel like leaving his warm flat to go out into the cold and sing for his supper. But it was Saturday and Christmas Eve, a good time to earn some extra cash. He thought it strange that the festive season still brought out that feeling of goodwill in people, they were certainly more generous.

The forecast said it would be very cold but dry so he had wrapped himself in several layers of clothing, put on a woollen hat and two pairs of socks. He was ready to move out and would be in Fram market square by eleven. He picked up his accordion and trudged up there.

Whilst walking his thoughts were glum and not helped by the cold grey weather. For the last six months he had been waiting to hear something positive from Adrian, the guy who had praised his talent and said he would try to help him. But he had only had one call a couple of months after their meeting. He had been told that things were progressing but there had been no update since. His thoughts turned to rhyming,

Now it's a bummer, when hope in summer

Don't come to fruition, but stifles my ambition

He said I had a gift, and that he would give me a lift

Enhance my profile and market my style

But I haven't heard, not had the word......

His thoughts were interrupted when he heard someone shouting his name.

'Jim. Jim!'

He turned and saw George, the barman from The Castle running up the road behind him.

He reached Jim, panting from his exertions. 'I thought it was you. Well it had to be. Not many people carry an accordion case. You're looking a bit down in the dumps.'

'Yeah. Well it's Christmas and I don't feel festive.'

'You're not going to make much if you don't put on a smile.'

Jim gave him a big beaming false smile.

'That's better. I know you'll want to play two or three hours in the square, but make sure you get to the pub for two. You might find it useful '

'Find what useful. What's it about?'

'Just get there for two and I'll let you know. Have a little patience. I'm sure it will interest you, one way or the other, but I haven't time to discuss it now. I've got a pub to get ready for a busy lunchtime. See you later.'

'Give me a clue!'

George shook his head and walked off leaving Jim puzzled. However he had every intention of being at the pub on time and would be ready for a bit of warmth and refreshment after three hours in the square.

The town centre was as busy as he expected and the market stalls were doing good business. He set himself up near the centre of the square and started playing some Christmas tunes on the accordion. People passed and deposited coins in the wooden box in front of him.

'Thank you and merry Christmas!'

The box was filling up, but he was getting bored and decided to try his Framgnam rap.

'Christmas is here – you're full of cheer - you listen to me - you know it's free - but still you give – and help me live - in a style I fit - waiting for that hit - Will it come or not - Will I get a chart spot? - Now I see you smile - you like my style - you're all good folk - and I don't joke - A genuine guy - look in my eye - See my smile – and listen a while - then float my boat – with a coin or note.'

Jim then went onto playing 'We Wish You A Merry Christmas' on his accordion and coins were dropped into his box by those who had been listening. He noted they we largely pound coins and smiled.

It had been about two and a half hours and he reckoned that he had made about thirty five pounds. He decided to pack up and go up to the Castle to find out what George had to say. Walking into the bar he found it still heaving with Christmas revellers so he stood at the bar trying to catch George's eye, which was not easy. Eventually he got George's attention and he came across.

'Hi Jim. I hadn't realised you would get here this early, I have to keep helping behind the bar whilst it's busy. It should start to slow down in the next half hour. Have a pint and I'll come across when it calms down.'

Jim stood at the bar sipping his pint and luxuriating in the warmth. He looked around and spotted some regulars, but most of the folk seemed to be shoppers getting into the Christmas mood having completed their shopping. He mused as he looked on;

They got their toys, they got their grub,
The girls and boys sit in the pub.
It's Christmas and they're getting with it,
With love and peace, beer and spirit.
Down it goes with unthinking ease.
Barman I'll have another please.

'Jim I can talk now.' There was no response. 'Jim!'

'Oh sorry George I was deep in thought. So tell me what it's about.'

'Well I got a call from Adrian. He wanted to run something by me and if I thought it was okay he asked if I'd have a chat with you. So here I am.'

'I don't understand. Why didn't he call me?'

'He thought it needed a personal discussion but wasn't able to make it up here. Adrian's a friend from school and knows he can trust me.'

'I'm still puzzled but go on.'

George told him about the conversation with Adrian. He had apologised for the delay but explained that there was interest from various club owners in London.

'That's great. Sign me up. I still don't see why he couldn't phone me.'

'Well there is a catch. The fact is that most of the interest came from gay clubs.'

Jim stared at George trying to take in what had been said and then exploded.

'What!! You want me to entertain a load of nancy boys!'

'Well you know that Adrian took some snaps of you when you were wearing those leathers and shades. That and the quirky accordion music and rap touched a chord in the gay clubs.'

Jim stared at George dumbstruck.

'I know it's a shock, but it is a good opportunity. There is a big gay community and all major cities have gay venues. Some of the London clubs have links to clubs in the US, particularly Vegas. In fact Adrian thinks you could be in Vegas within a year.'

'What! Hang on, go slow. Firstly I am not gay or bisexual. The leathers are sometimes part of the act and I thought it was a cool look, not a gay look. I repeat I am not gay.'

George laughed. 'You doth protest too

much!'

Jim gave him an evil stare.

'Seriously Jim, you don't need to be gay and you don't need to act gay. Just be yourself. Adrian thinks it's a great opportunity. He will manage you, fix the venues et cetera. All you have to do is get on stage and do your stuff and be paid good money. What do you say?'

Jim continued to stare at him, not saying a word. After a while he spoke cautiously.

'Okay. I think I can get over the gay thing. But where do I stay. I can't afford to live in London.'

'Adrian's thought of that. You know he's loaded and he's prepared to put you up in his apartment.'

'That's very good of him. Is he gay?'

'Get over the gay thing. It could be a great opportunity for you. Adrian reckons he can get some good slots for you in January. Yes or no?'

Jim gave a big sigh.

'Oh bugger it! Tell him it's a yes.'

'Let's have a drink and celebrate.'

George poured two scotches and raised his glass.

'Happy Christmas. Here's to your success.'

Jim raised his glass.

'Happy Christmas, George! I'll let you know when I'm off to Vegas'

FAMILY TREE
Will Ingrams

If I had to be stuffed, shrunk
and stuck on a Christmas tree
I wouldn't want the budded top,
impaled as an imperious fairy
or a glass-hearted star.
I'd hate to hang
from a sticky branch tip
fearing festive wags of
the daft dog's agitated tail,
found fallen in
unhoovered rough
from a party-dress's
boisterous brush.

Behind tinsel-glints and
soft slow corona glow
I would hide in thick
spike-dark shadows near
the rough-cut resined trunk
inhaling pine and
orange peel memories,
storing slippery slices

of unsaid togetherness,
ephemeral instants
of sibling forgiveness
and everyday
well-concealed love.

CHRISTMAS IS NOT FOR DOGS
Anne Foster-Clarke

The days are getting shorter,
it's dark so very soon
And when she takes me for my walk
we can sometimes see the moon.
But I know her mind is elsewhere,
she's busy making plans.
She's thinking 'bout buying presents,
baking, using pots and pans.

She's got the festive CD's out,
the noise of carols rock our house.
The din, it is tremendous,
and would frighten any mouse.
She dragged this tree in yesterday and set it
in my corner. She's moved my bed
And in its stead I've fairy lights and angels
hanging just above my head.

Christmas Eve, she's filling stockings,
there's no time left for me.
She's icing cakes, the stuffings done.
'Oi, what about my tea?' I shout in desperation.
I get a dish of biscuits with giblets on the side.
Then I'm plonked between two smart phones
and a bicycle to ride.

Christmas Day is here again,
the village bells, they're ringing
Cousins, Aunts, and family
they're all in church a-singing.
But I'm all right, I've got my mates.
Big Stan and curly Mai.
We're just about to trash the place.
This dog will have his day!

By Frank the Jack Russell, Stanley the
Labrador and Maisie the Lakeland Terrier

A BIT OF WINTER
WARMTH
Joan Roberts

Ruby stands by the window in a daydream. The sky threatens more snow and treacherous ice still clings to the pavements at two in the afternoon. The heavy overcoats worn by the few passers-by is a clear warning to all those who might venture forth. Ruby pulls her cardigan closer around her shoulders. There are patches of dark ground where cars were parked overnight. The noise of early morning departures now a distant reminder that twice a day at least the street is alive with activity as drivers jostle for the limited spaces. The only sound is the grumbling traffic as it groans its way along the motorway nearby and a cat who begs to be allowed to share the warmth of the inside of one of the terraced houses that have lined the street for nearly 10 decades.

Three or four of the houses are boarded up. Damp and decay have taken their toll. They await a new future, or maybe demolition. The tenants, now long gone, remembered as good friends in harder times. Like two lines of soldiers the houses face each other on parade. Over the years, the inhabitants have changed the tone of the street. Old timers make way for the younger commuters who start their married life here then move to more substantial houses when the babies begin to arrive. These days there is more diversity as one after another the houses are transformed to suit their new owners. Some have smart new windows and doors, white plastic, double glazing, brass or chrome door knockers and numbers. All have TV aerials. Many satellite dishes adorn the street like posh hats, or huge fans just sticking out above a top floor window. So different from when they were tied -houses for the workers of Henshaw's Mill. Often two large families would cram the limited space of four small rooms and share the tiny privy in the back yard. The inevitable zinc bath, which doubled as wash tub for families and their clothes, hung on the back wall. No running hot water then. The coal, fireplaces and chimneys now vanquished, with the soot and the smog it created.

At the end of the street the dormant gasometer stands like a skeletal giant space craft who waits for instruction from its mother ship to leave its post that dominates the skyline. Then the quiet shatters momentarily as the 14.33 to Piccadilly thunderously approaches the railway bridge, the two houses below shudder as the engine and its carriages screech their way forward.

A red van drives into the street and pulls up outside an empty house, old Mary Porter's house, poor old thing. A large man with dark skin and a beard gets out of the van and zips his coat and pulls his hood up to cover the small white dome-shaped hat on his head. He goes to the back of the van and opens the doors wide. Another old, white hatch-back pulls up behind with another man, a woman and some small children. A phone rings and Ruby turns away from her window to answer it.

'Oh Jack. I've just been looking outside to see if I dare go out. The snow's still on the ground. I need some more bread and tea.' She listens while her son explains how it would be impossible now for him to come and collect her for Christmas as they'd planned. Lauren has not been well, and Jimmy is in the school play, Lauren's mother, etc. etc. She's heard it all before.

'Yes, of course I understand. What is wrong with Lauren?' Jack's wife Lauren was always suffering from some ailment or other when Ruby was due to visit. 'Well I hope she's better soon. Give my love to Jimmy and wish him luck in his play.' She would so like to see him. She couldn't remember how long ago it had been, he'll be a big boy now. 'Yes dear. Remember me to Lauren's mother. It would be nice if you could phone on Christmas day with Jimmy.' She puts down the phone taking a deep breath to dispel her disappointment. and goes through to the kitchen. One teabag. She will have to brace herself for the elements.

Ruby curses herself for not shopping yesterday as she steps with great trepidation through the front door. She manoeuvres the trolley out behind her and over the step. She doesn't have that much to get, but the trolley is such a blessing and gives her so much support she rarely goes anywhere without it these days. Suddenly the ground runs away from her as she slips. She claws frantically at thin air to no avail and lands on the icy, wet pavement, her arm caught awkwardly underneath her. She feels stupid, embarrassed, and the pain from her trapped arm is excruciating. The man from the red van hurries over.

'I have called to my wife. Please stay where you are. You will be very shaken.'

A young woman in a headscarf and warm overcoat comes over and bends down and speaks.

'I am Aala.' Ruby surprised by her strong Manchester accent, tries to smile back. 'You took a nasty tumble, didn't you? Where does it hurt? No please don't move. Rab, please go over and get the hall mat and we'll try and get her on to that. And call an ambulance.' Aala turned back to Ruby who begins to feel very sick. 'I think you have hurt your arm, haven't you and we need to get you in a warm place very quickly. I can't offer you tea I'm afraid we have no electricity yet.' Rab and another man come over with a rug and Ruby is gently but firmly rearranged onto the mat and covered with a duvet. Then she passes out.

Ruby is aware of someone holding her hand, a woman. She opens her eyes and sees Aala's kind face smiling at her. She squeezes Ruby's hand and calls the nurse over. The nurse, who doesn't really seem much younger than Ruby, gives her a stern look.

'Well you've given us a right old time my dear. Your arm is broken and a nasty bruise on your leg so it looks like your dancing will be limited this Christmas.'

'How long have you been here?' said Ruby to Aala. 'I honestly don't know what happened now.' The nurse motions to Aala to move away from the bed and draws round the curtains.

'She's been here ages. Told her there was nothing to do but she wouldn't leave you. Don't worry about your purse and bag, it's in the side cupboard.' This said in a low, conspiratorial voice. 'I'll get it out when I've finished the vitals and you can check it's all there.' Ruby tries ignore the inference in the nurse's tone, but she becomes aware of her plaster caste arm and suddenly of a nasty ache around the top of her leg. She feels thoroughly miserable. Christmas is going to be the worst one since Syd died eight years ago.

Ruby stays in hospital for days. Everyday Aala comes to visit her. She brings her grapes and oranges and chats about how they're settling in to their new home. She asks Ruby if she should call Jack. Ruby tries to explain that Jack might not be too happy about having to make such a journey because he has such a busy job.

When Aala leaves Ruby is approached by a very imperious nurse who introduces herself as the OP. Ruby is uncertain whether to ask what this means but realises that her future may be decided for her if she is unable to make plans.

'I believe you have a son, will it be possible for him to take care of you? If not then we will have to contact social care and see what they can do for you. It's such a difficult time of year. We really need the beds.' Ruby didn't want to stay in the hospital, but knew she would struggle at home on her own. She had been out of bed now several times and could walk with difficulty, but her right arm was going to be in a caste for several weeks which would make any kind of housework difficult. She was sure that she would struggle to shop too.

'Hello Ruby,' says Aala as she pulls up a chair the next day.

'Will you not be with your son for Christmas? I'm sure if I was to explain what has happened he would want to come up to be with you, or take you back to his home.'

Ruby smiles at Aala. What a lovely girl she is. Very pretty, always a lovely smile and such a caring lass. How different from Jack's Lauren. Lauren somehow found smiling very difficult, and Ruby was convinced that she was devoid of any sensitivity.

'If you were to ring him, *she* would be up here like a shot. Rummaging through everything to see what she could sell. Then they'd sell the house and put me in a home.' There, she'd said it out loud. Aala's face was full of concern.

'Oh, I'm sure…' she stops midsentence. 'If you hadn't had the accident, what would you have done at Christmas, since you weren't going to spend it with your family?'

'I suppose I would have made myself a little dinner, chicken and stuffing. Settled down in front of the telly. There's a Carol concert at the Church, Christmas Eve. They have a lovely choir and the vicar always has a little tea after with his lost lambs; us few old 'uns that can still get about. Last year there were some young kids, refugees, or asylum seekers, not sure which. They were good fun. Didn't speak much English but the confusion caused a bit of a hoot. Especially since some of us have bad hearing problems anyway.' She pauses, smiling, at the memory of one or two moments she had been really touched. A little boy who had been traumatised by something he'd witnessed, he hadn't spoken a word since he'd arrived. He'd started to laugh and clap as she did her version of Have you seen the Muffin Man? whilst balancing a glass of orange juice on her head. She done it with a pint of beer in the old days to make Jack laugh.

'I'll have to see what social care come up with, Aala. I hope it's not a home. I don't think I could bear that.'

After Aala leaves, Ruby walks down to the day room. Countdown is on the TV and Ruby sits to watch it. Looking around the room there are several old people, some of them watching, one asleep. Ruby shudders. *Is this my future?*

Next day all is hustle and bustle. Ruby is told that there's been a major incident on the motorway and that the wards are filling up with casualties all over the hospital. Aala appears at visiting time. She has nothing with her and she seems in a bit of a hurry.

'My youngest is off with a really bad cough, my niece is watching him for me so I can't stop long.'

'You shouldn't have worried about me Aala. You're so good to put yourself out for me. You barely know me, after all.'

'Well the truth is that you are about the same age as my mum and there's something about you that reminds me of her.' She laughs at the expression on Ruby's face. 'No, not in looks. But she fell, just like you, only she didn't recover. I'm afraid she had a massive heart attack and died.' Her eyes cloud over and Ruby reaches out and takes her hand. 'It's funny the things you remember. It all came back to me when I saw you there, on the pavement. But it was a long time ago now, and my Dad had to work so I practically brought up my younger sister and brother. Anyway, that's all in the past. I've come to tell you that Rab and I would love it if you'll let us take you home to your house, and I 'd be happy to come over to see you every day until you are better to make sure there is someone to keep an eye on you. Rab has said if you are well he will drive you to the Church on Christmas Eve so that you can be with the other lambs.'

Aala is as good as her word and two days later Rab comes to pick her up and take her home. The look on the faces of some of the other patients is something that makes Ruby smile every time she thinks of it afterwards. He and Aala settle her in and made her something to eat.

'Later, I'll come back and get your dinner, or you could join us if you are up to crossing the road? The snow has been gone for some time.'

'You're going to so much trouble. I must be putting you out.'

'Not at all, I'll ask my niece to call in after school and she'll be happy to escort you across or let me know to come to you.' Aala's face beamed at her. 'It's nothing I wouldn't have done for my Mum and it gives me such pleasure.' Ruby is so touched that she holds back a little sob. The telephone rings and as she reaches to answer Rab and Aala point to the door and leave.

'Hallo Jack. How are you and how is Lauren?' She listens intently as Jack explains that he's calling her now as the next few days are going to be very busy and they are going to Lauren's mother for Christmas, as Lauren was feeling so much better, and he's not sure when he might have time to call.

'Is Billy there?' she asks. Jack explains the problems with teenagers and how busy things are for them, with after school activities and friends and dress rehearsals etc. Ruby looks across at the last photograph of Billy on the mantelpiece, he was about seven. She hadn't seen him now for about two years, a more recent photograph would be nice. 'Yes, I understand. Perhaps there will be some photos from the play? You must let me know how he gets on. Perhaps you'll be able to get up in the New Year?' Of course, the problems of the New Year, the weather, the traffic, Lauren's mother. She wondered whether to tell him of her fall but then thought better of it. She would hate him to accuse her of emotional blackmail. So, she wishes him all the usual greetings. Ruby reassures him that she will be fine. Why ask? she thinks. You don't really care! She puts down the phone and cries like a baby.

Going to Aala's in the evening for dinner is a regular thing by Christmas Eve. Ruby is amazed at the food that is very different from what she would have cooked herself, and enjoys it far more than she'd anticipated. The other members of the family are delightful and Aala's niece Asafa, soon becomes a great companion too. Asafa calls in the following weekend to learn to knit and crochet under Ruby's watchful eye. The Christmas Eve party is a huge success and many of the refugees have returned. This year though, despite much begging from one little boy, 'Have you seen the Muffin Man?' is shelved, until maybe next year.

When Christmas Day arrives, Ruby finds herself invited to Aala and Rab's for Lunch and the most untraditional Christmas Day. There is no Christmas tree, but plenty of decorations. Instead of sitting in front of a TV watching repeats of old shows, there is laughter and stories from Rab about his country and his memories as a little boy. They all sing songs together. There are solos too, from Taai, Aala's eldest boy who has a beautiful voice. Ruby sings Somewhere over the Rainbow which is well received and they all sing together some songs from Mary Poppins. It is a wonderful day.

As Ruby draws her curtains in her bedroom that night, she sees lights on up and down the street as people continue to watch their televisions and there is laughter and music as Christmas parties continue. A plane flies overhead and there is still a faint rumble from the motorway beyond.

Ruby settles into bed and ponders on her next call from Jack. She hasn't thought about him all day. She decides to tell him about the fall and what a wonderful friend she's discovered because of it.

A cat screams and there is a loud hiss from another as they fight among the tightly parked cars. How different her life has become in just a few weeks? Snuggling down she feels a warm glow all over.

Thank you for reading our book.
If you enjoyed **Bright Stars in a Big Sky** we would
be so grateful if you could find the time to leave a
review.

Many thanks.

BigSky Writers

Other Books by BigSky Writers

Beneath a Big Sky

Amazon: http://getBook.at/beneathabi

Spectrum

Amazon: http://getBook.at/spectrum

Made in the USA
Columbia, SC
29 October 2017